A Prope _____

While Dionne focused the video camera, Amber started interviewing me. "Cher, what kind of high school boy would you consider dating?"

It was a provocative question. I let my gaze roam across the Quad. "Okay, so," I began, scanning the crowd for even minimally doable dating material. "What kind of high school boy would I—"

Suddenly a beam of sunlight sliced through the L.A. haze, wondrously illuminating a Baldwinian stranger making his way through the random crowd. I was struck dumb. But only momentarily.

"That kind!" I exclaimed, transfixed by the lean and lanky hottie's clean looks, classic poise, and chronic fashion sense. He was sheathed in the exact same silver suit that Leonardo DiCaprio had just been photographed in for like either *Details* or *Vanity Fair*.

De followed my gaze and gasped. "Who is that?"

"The Baldwin from another planet," I whispered reverently.

Clueless™ Books

CLUELESS™
A novel by H. B. Gilmour
Based on the film written and directed by
Amy Heckerling

CLUELESS™: CHER'S GUIDE TO . . . WHATEVER
By H. B. Gilmour

CLUELESS™: ACHIEVING PERSONAL PERFECTION
By H. B. Gilmour

CLUELESS™: AN AMERICAN BETTY IN PARIS
By Randi Reisfeld

CLUELESS™: CHER NEGOTIATES NEW YORK
By Jennifer Baker

CLUELESS™: CHER'S FURIOUSLY FIT WORKOUT
By Randi Reisfeld

CLUELESS™: FRIEND OR FAUX
By H. B. Gilmour

CLUELESS™: CHER GOES ENVIRO-MENTAL
By Randi Reisfeld

CLUELESS™: BALDWIN FROM ANOTHER PLANET
By H. B. Gilmour

Available from ARCHWAY Paperbacks

CLUELESS™

Baldwin from Another Planet

H.B. Gilmour

AN ARCHWAY PAPERBACK
Published by POCKET BOOKS
New York London Toronto Sydney Tokyo Singapore

This book is a work of fiction. Names, characters, places and
incidents are products of the author's imagination or are used
fictitiously. Any resemblance to actual events or locales or persons,
living or dead, is entirely coincidental.

AN ARCHWAY PAPERBACK *Original*

 An Archway Paperback published by
POCKET BOOKS, a division of Simon & Schuster Inc.
1230 Avenue of the Americas, New York, NY 10020

™ and Copyright © 1997 by Paramount Pictures

ISBN: 0-671-00325-9

First Archway Paperback printing March 1997

10 9 8 7 6 5 4 3 2 1

AN ARCHWAY PAPERBACK and colophon are
registered trademarks of Simon & Schuster Inc.

Printed in the U.S.A.

IL: 7+

With love and gratitude to
Doris, Amira, the great Greenberg,
dearest John, and, always, Jess

Baldwin
from Another Planet

Chapter 1

"Cher, I totally don't get what all this has to do with Ralph Lauren," my best friend, De, remarked. We and our couturely challenged bud, Amber, had gotten ourselves excused from P.E. and were sunning in the bleachers while our less fortunate classmates galloped by.

It was Friday afternoon, last period, time for Ms. Stoeger's phys ed class. Today's team sport: polo. As in sweaty horses, coif-crushing helmets, and stretch jodhpurs that balloon at the thigh. All thanks to our classmate Annabell Gutterman's father, the polo fanatic, who had donated a gazillion dollars to Bronson Alcott High to promote the sport.

I gazed at the mallet-waving girls bouncing painfully past on brutally high-strung ponies. "Polo is a sport, De," I tried to explain. "And where it interfaces with

1

Ralph is that it tends to draw the same type of people who go for his faux bunkhouse look. Plus polo ponies are way expensive."

Sporting a stiff new winged hairdo and a wide-shouldered suit, Amber swung the video camera she was holding from Dionne to me. "So you're saying, Cher," she announced, "that the synergy between the sport and Ralph is like what? Saddle Sores of the Rich and Famous?"

Amber, who sees herself as a fashion trendsetter, had put together what she thought of as a Leeza Gibbons–Cindy Crawford TV newscaster kind of look, accessorized by a cute little Minicam in a Vuitton carrying case.

"Excuse me, Amber," I said. "Unless you're doing a training film for student dermatologists, could you not videotape me in extreme close-up?"

"It's not even on," she replied. Then the three of us shrieked and ducked as a mallet sailed into the stands.

"Oops!" Baez called, clutching her horse's mane and shrugging apologetically.

"Oops?" De raged as the long-handled wooden hammer clattered down the bleachers and out of harm's way. "Is that what Dennis Rodman's hair colorist said or what? 'Oops' is *such* a brutal understatement."

I caught Amber's camera, which flew from her hands as she protectively grabbed her surgically enhanced nose. Then I lifted my new Web shades and stared in disbelief at the near-lethal mallet. It was lying defused now on the lush AstroTurf below.

Somewhat shaken by our near-death experience, the three of us abandoned the bleachers.

"Does this thing really work?" I asked Amber, examining the video cam. We were leisurely wending our way from the school sports complex toward the coed congestion of the Quad.

"How should I know? I just picked it up at Nordstrom because it totally goes with my savvy-chic anchorperson threads," Amber explained, twirling to display her latest look.

In addition to a Pooh backback, Amber's costume consisted of five-inch stiletto-heeled Manolo slingbacks, a layered silk miniskirt with matching vinyl jacket, and this strangely textured sweater that looked more like cat hair than cashmere. Not one of your pedigreed breeds, either.

"You're no Tom Brokaw," I said.

"Thanks," Amber replied as Dionne took the video cam from me and clicked on the power.

"Excellent," De said. "It works. Let's do a real interview."

"This is so perfect." Amber dug into her backback for hairspray. "And I am so perfect." Oblivious to ecological concerns, she shpritzed a mist of super-hold at her already stiff red-tinted coiffure. "Do you even know how dressed for news-anchor success I am? I just need like an idea . . . you know, for a segment, a live spot. What should I cover?"

As if to say "Your hair?" De cocked her head at Amber's helmet of henna but exercised excellent verbal restraint. I was way proud of her. Amber, however, had noticed the look.

"Fully amusing," she responded, applying a fresh

slick of gloss to her gleaming red lips. "I guess if I didn't have a clue, I'd do something furiously childish to cover up my feelings of inadequacy, too."

"Ooooh, listen to the girlfriend snappin' on your woman."

"Yo, yo, Dionne, was you doggin' the sister?"

As these witty remarks wafted across the lawn to us, we turned to confront Bronson Alcott's masculine answer to Salt-N-Pepa, the sartorial soul mates of the Hilfiger-Nautica nexus: Dionne's boyfriend, Murray, and his best friend, Sean.

De rolled her classic hazel eyes at them. "How droll, Murray, or do you prefer 'How totally fly'? As usual, your command of colorful street slang is way impressive. And furiously useful, too. Especially if you're planning to apply to like . . . the University of McDonald's."

"Like ha-ha," Amber added. "If it isn't the Wayans brothers, drastically reduced for clearance."

Sean made a major event of turning his sun visor sideways. Murray's gold-accented grin glinted in the sunlight. "Props given to homeboy humor and its irrefutable impact on pop culture," he declared. Then, cackling and slapping high fives, the men of Bronson Alcott continued their stroll across campus.

"Now, there's a subject I could discuss ad hurleam," I said, "the appalling scarcity of seriously evolved males in our world."

We came to a stone bench situated near a glade of palmettos and furiously flowering hibiscus. Our school grounds are way better groomed than our boy population.

"Excellent." Amber was pleased with my topic. "Let's sit down here. I'll interview you, and De can tape us."

Which is just what we did after I refreshed my lip tint and shook out my long, shimmering blond locks. With De behind the Minicam, Amber stuck her face in front of the lens. "So, Cher," she began, tilting her head to convey rapt curiosity. Her stiff hair crackled audibly as she moved. "Tell us why you haven't had a decent date since you started high school?"

"First of all, Amber," I replied, signaling for De to focus the camera on me, "I'd like to rephrase your question. Like if you're asking my opinion on the current crop of boys at this and other high schools in the greater Beverly Hills area, I'd have to say subsidies are way overdue. Like the crop, so to speak, is failing. There's a total Baldwin famine on the land."

"Cut. Cut!" Amber hollered, reaching out and clicking off the camera. "Cher, we're talking males here, not alfalfa. What is all this 'crop' stuff?"

"Excuse me. Have you ever even heard of metaphor?" I asked.

"She probably thinks it's one less than meta-five," De suggested.

Amber flashed her an excuse-me look. "Duh, of course I know what a metaphor is." She was deeply affronted. "Like I didn't negotiate up from a C-minus to a B-plus in English last semester? I was just hoping for a more frontal approach to the topic. Like basically, let's focus on the Crew. I mean, they're supposed to be the most desirable hotties on campus—"

"Okay, De, start again," I said.

5

Dionne stood up on the bench and pointed the camera down at me. "Oh, this is a great angle," she called. "Like there's no chin sag whatsoever."

"Dionne, I am fifteen years old and fully toned!"

"Okay, we're rolling," she said. "I'm taping this now."

"All right," I said. "Take for instance the Crew. As Bronson Alcott boys go, they are supposedly the best and the brightest. Yet does even one of them subscribe to *GQ* or *Uomo*? Do they ever like hold open a door for anyone, be it car or cafeteria? And speaking of cafeteria, is there a man among them who hasn't like laughed food products out through his nose and grossed out an entire table, let alone spewed latte on the innocent? Okay, so they'll throw the occasional excellent bender when one or more parents do a cross-coastal or otherwise temporarily evacuate a casa. And generally they're physically fit, with a few sporting really attractive cuts. But when they try to make conversation . . . I mean, witness the scintillating exchange we just had with Sean and Murray—and they're like smart!" I paused and flipped back my hair. "So how does that look?" I asked De.

"Majorly choice. This is way more entertaining than *Algebra for Everyone* and *Africa: A Continent in Transition*," she said, citing the TV fare currently airing on Bronson Alcott's new closed-circuit video channel.

"I don't know," Amber objected, sticking her head back into camera range. "I think we should aim for a more solution-oriented approach. Like, Cher, what kind of high school boy would you consider dating?"

It was a provocative question. I let my gaze roam across the Quad. Eighth period was nearly over. Kids had begun to pour out the doors, tossing crumpled paper balls at one another, applying gel to their hair, adjusting their body rings, speed-dialing their cell phones, shouting, skateboarding, and searching their backpacks for their valet parking tickets.

"Okay, so," I began, scanning the crowd for even minimally doable dating material. "What kind of high school boy would I—"

Suddenly a beam of sunlight sliced through the L.A. haze, wondrously illuminating a Baldwinian stranger making his way through the random crowd. I was struck dumb. But only momentarily.

"That kind!" I exclaimed, transfixed by the lean and lanky hottie's clean looks, classic poise, and chronic fashion sense. He was sheathed in the exact same silver suit that Leonardo DiCaprio had just been photographed in for like either *Details* or *Vanity Fair*.

De followed my gaze and gasped. "Who is that?"

"The Baldwin from another planet," I whispered reverently. "I mean, outside of *W*'s menswear supplement, I've never seen an earthling packaged so properly."

Amber turned too. "I've never seen him before, either. But I saw that outfit when Elsa Klensch covered the Milan fashion scene for CNN," she shrieked. "It's so next year and totally Italian."

De scrambled off the bench, and the three of us stood there, trying not to stare slack-jawed at the stylish hunk heading our way.

He had thick slicked-back streaky-blond hair with these rebellious runaway locks that curled behind his ears and kind of flopped over his forceful brow. "Ciao," he called, with this opulent smile aimed directly at me. "I look for the office. Is this way?"

"I knew it!" Amber yelled triumphantly. "You're Italian, right?"

His facial details were excellently organized: a way decent nose, properly sculpted lips, and a fully noble jaw. Yet his dark eyes managed to look vulnerable, and his skin had this velvety boyish blush.

Tossing back a stray strand of hair, he shrugged modestly. "My accent give me away, yes?"

"No," Amber assured him. "Your suit. It's bitterly golden . . . as silver suits go. I saw it on the runway—"

"Speaking of runways," De burst in, "are you a model?"

His full lips parted, revealing this seriously adorable space between his front teeth. "No, no." He laughed. "No way. I go to school. Here. If I can find the office. I go to register." He turned back to me. "My name is Aldo," he said. "Aldo Belloguardia. And you?"

Vastly relieved that I'd had a chipped juliette repaired a mere forty-eight hours ago, I extended my hand. Maintenance is a major beauty tool. "Cher Horowitz," I said.

"Cher." Aldo grasped my hand in both of his. *"Bella.* Very beautiful."

"And I'm Amber. Which is also a prime name, don't you think? I'm a furiously devoted fan of Italian couture," she informed him, stepping between us. "I'm practically the only girl I know who can like actually spell Enzo Angiolini and Ermenegildo Zegna, let alone recognize their superb craftsmanship. Also, I'm five feet six inches in pedicured bare feet, one hundred pounds—"

"Not counting hair," De murmured. "Hi, Aldo, I'm Dionne. You can call me De."

"The office is over there, Aldo." Amber pointed across De's face, her vinyl sleeve rudely obstructing Dionne's gracious smile.

"*Grazie*. Thank you." Bruisingly noble eyes locked longingly on mine for a moment. "So . . . *arrivederci*. I see you soon again, yes? Ciao." With a final flash of that adorable grin, Aldo headed for the registrar's office.

De ducked under Amber's arm. "Welcome to Bronson Alcott High," she called after him. "I'm sure you'll find our school extremely enriching." Then she gave me this look. "And vice versa," she said.

Chapter 2

An hour later De, Amber, and I were at the mall, cruising the carpeted aisles of Neiman Marcus. Although our arms were braceleted with shopping bags, we weren't seriously concentrating on our mission. I mean, okay, each of us had acquired a few interesting items, but nothing that would actually send parental blood pressure soaring or require complicated explanations.

Caught up in excited conversation, we moved from cosmetic counter to cosmetic counter, barely noticing the new scents being shpritzed onto our upturned wrists. By the time we got to swimwear, it was clear that Aldo Belloguardia beat out even the thirty-percent-off bikini sale as the high-interest event of the day.

"I cannot believe the way he looked at you," Amber

was saying, holding up a skimpy feathered animal-print suit.

She'd handed De her Pooh backpack and me the video cam.

"Too primitive," I said, studying her through the lens.

"*Au contraire*, Cher. I thought the boy was frantically civilized," De commented.

"Not Aldo. Amber's swimwear," I explained.

"Actually, there *was* something primitive about him." Amber allowed herself a dramatic shudder. "Is that thing on?" She pointed to the video camera. I nodded, and she perked up considerably.

"Those piercing dark eyes," she continued, tossing the feathered suit over her shoulder to a waiting salesperson. The poor woman's shoulders and arms were festooned with swimwear that Amber had discarded. Littered with castoffs, she looked like a designer scarecrow.

As De, Amber, and I strolled across the aisle to lingerie, I directed the video cam at the patient saleslady. She was returning Amber's rejects to the rack. One of the bikinis Amber had pitched to her bore a classic Simona Biagi pattern. Biagi is a brutally famous fabric designer who does way whimsical things with cotton. So I zoomed in on this particular bathing suit, and then I pulled back for a fuller view of the salesperson.

All at once she stumbled forward and crashed into the rack of swimwear. Then a woman a few feet away from her started shrieking. And suddenly another customer shouted and tumbled from view.

"Is there like an earthquake happening on the other side of the aisle?" De asked.

"Everyone in swimwear is totally toppling," I said.

"Let's bail!" Amber cried, stepping over both pieces of an Anna Sui plaid bikini that had spilled from the fallen saleslady's arms. "This store is total chaos—and furiously noisy. I mean, like even the store personnel are screaming."

"We can do a caffeine break and continue our Aldo analysis at the food court," De proposed, grabbing my arm and tugging me toward the entrance of the store.

I handed the video cam to Dionne. "Take me exiting, okay?"

Amber and I hurried ahead of Dionne while she filmed. At the glass doors we paused to wave at the camera. Then Amber sauntered out of the store. I was standing in the doorway, giving De that extra little "Okay, we're Audi," when this burly stooge in totally bogus signature jeans—like Gitano rip-offs, which is so why bother?—and a grossly bulging faux-leather jacket came barreling toward me.

I could not believe my eyes. The guy was carrying a purse. I mean, it was burgundy alligator and looked extremely authentic. Which, aside from ecological considerations, meant it cost more than his entire ensemble, including the oversize yet underwhelming gold medallion he was sporting and these tawdry motorcycle boots with decorative spurs.

I was sure he would halt or at least pause. I was standing right there, blatantly visible in my canary yellow crop-top cardigan. The man could so not have failed to see me. But did he consider stopping? Not even. He crashed right into me. And suddenly this explosion of designer wallets, change purses, and credit cards burst from his tacky jacket.

The next thing I knew, he was gone. And I was sailing out into the mall, skidding across these tawdry terrazzo tiles—that people walk on!—fully sprawled in my favorite lemon linen slacks.

As Amber rushed to my aid, I shouted at the poster boy for the rude, "Excuse me. Do you even know how ill-mannered that is?"

As if! A man in an erupting plastic jacket and cheesy imitation jeans is not your basic etiquette buff. Plus he didn't even know that too much conditioner makes thinning hair look just plain greasy.

Dionne came running out of the store, video camera in hand. "Are you okay?"

I stood up and brushed myself off. "Did you get all that? Did you see that tasteless individual assault me?"

"He's a wanted purse-snatcher, Cher. He's been terrorizing this entire mall," De reported. "The store security guard told me. The guy snagged a ton of valuables before he got away."

"Was he carrying a Lana Marks bag?" Amber asked.

"Burgundy alligator," I said. "I saw it, too. It was so cute."

"Did you get a good look at him?" De wanted to know.

"Dionne," I said, "he was so close I could smell his aftershave—which is probably sold by the keg."

"I've got this total brainstorm." Amber got all excited. "Give me the camera."

"Amber, it is way too late to videotape the felon in flight." De handed over the Minicam. "He's probably in the parking lot by now, hot-wiring Suburbans or whatever."

"Also," I said, "he is so not photogenic."

"Not him, you," Amber said. "This is a way decent op to do one of those on-the-spot crime-scene reports— you know, with all these generic individuals waving to their moms behind you. It'll be so fun. De, you do the anchor thing, okay?"

I hardly had a chance to repair my gloss before De went like "We're here at the mall with Cher Horowitz, a personal witness to today's heinous designer purse-snatching. Cher, in your own words, can you describe what happened?"

"Of course," I said. "We were inside, scoping swimwear. Neiman's was supposed to be having this mighty sale. But they only had like heifer sizes left. Which is such a rip-off. Because, like right, if you're a size eight or over, would you even consider a two-piece—"

This cadet in baggy Markie Mark retreads stuck his face in front of me and made like a V-sign to the camera. And of course his complete slacker backup crew started cheering and going like "Ay, ay. Whassup?"

Amber clicked off the camera. "People, people!" she shouted. "We are not going to continue unless you settle down."

Then naturally everyone started going "Whoa" and

"Oooooh." So Dionne gave them this dazzling smile. "Please," she added, with a doe-eyed look that turned them into whimpering puppies. "Thank you," she said. "Now, Cher, I frantically agree with you on the bathing suit front, but can you describe the assailant in question? You know, like height, weight, any special identifying features . . ."

"Well, I can say that he was an extremely self-involved individual and that if he used a personal shopper, she or he should be fired on the spot. Nothing he wore was helpful at all. I mean, he was totally not toned, which made his wearing that snug imitation leather jacket borderline gross. Keanu Reeves, with a great tan, could *maybe* get away with the look. And the man's hair was truly forget about it. If he paid two dollars for that styling, he was basically overcharged."

"Okay," Amber called. "That's excellent."

"Thank you, Cher." De gave me a limp-wristed high five and crowded me out of camera range. "From the mall, this is Dionne——"

Amber cut her off. "We're off the air. I'm out of tape."

"That was so choice!" De said.

"And an important public service, too." Amber tucked the Minicam into its carrying case and slung it over her shoulder. "I'm going to call Alana right now and see if her dad can get it on the news."

"That is such a fresh scheme," Dionne enthused as Amber fished her cellular out of her furry backpack. "As a major East Coast anchorperson, Alana's dad has monster influence in the network news arena. Plus

Alana owes Cher and me big-time because we did her color chart for her. She was wearing the worst possible season. Winter! And she is such an autumn—"

"Excuse me," I interrupted their high-level conference. "My dad happens to be a totally prominent attorney, and I'd like to remind you that I was the guest celeb on this little interview show. I guess that means I have some say in whether or not I want to go public with this tape."

De was surprised. "Cher, you were majorly articulate. You gave this classic description of the fugitive. I personally found your remarks acerbic yet witty."

"Plus," said Amber, punching Alana's digits into the mobile, "you were intimately involved in the crime. The way that Barney bumped into you undoubtedly slowed his flight—"

"And could conceivably aid in his apprehension," De added. "Girlfriend, you demonstrated full-on courage under fire. Why would you want to rain on your golden moment in the crime-stopping sun?"

"How about . . . there was no makeup person present. No licensed hairstylist on deck. I have no idea how my locks looked. I mean, was there sufficient shimmer and bounce for me to sign a release on this segment?"

"Can I be honest?" Amber asked.

"No!" De and I answered in unison. Amber has a black belt in insensitivity, which she often mistakes for constructive criticism.

"I have to think of Daddy's reputation as well as my own," I continued. "I can't in good conscience okay this video until I get some hard answers. Like did my hair look really, really choice?"

"Not as classic as Aldo's," De teased me, "but way beyond *90210* and *Baywatch* standards. Come on, girl-friend, your dad will be so proud of your close brush with criminal justice." Then she threw in the convincer. "And imagine Aldo turning on the tube tonight and catching you on prime time."

Chapter 3

*T*schal

By Sunday the culprit had been caught. And it was all because of our videotape.

Scenes from our mall segment aired on local stations all weekend long. They only used like a second of De's interview with me. (My hair looked flawless. Even the lip gloss, which I was basically just experimenting with, totally worked on the small screen.) But they like focused on the footage that I personally shot—of the swimwear saleswoman toppling over.

The purse-snatching stooge was visible right behind her. You could even see the sleazy dragon medallion on his chest and the alligator bag tucked under his arm. One of his neighbors at this trailer park outside of Encino recognized him and called the police.

As De had predicted, Daddy was furiously impressed

with the way I'd performed my civic duty. He said I was just like my mom, which is a total compliment. We were standing in front of this excellent oil painting of her that hangs in our domed entryway, just outside Daddy's study.

Mom is deceased, but her legacy of personal perfection and social responsibility lives on in me. In the portrait, she's fully decked out in disco gear, which is making a fierce comeback among today's designers. As a do-gooder herself, I think Mom would have been pleased with this trend toward recycling. She had rampant respect for all living things and gave her fur coats the opportunity to hibernate for at least one season every year in cold storage. Which I find very moving.

"Did you know that the greater L.A. business alliance was offering a reward for this character?" Daddy asked.

Actually, the police had informed us of this unexpected bonus. I'd already allocated my portion. "Yes, isn't it an excellent coincidence?" I said. "It'll totally cover the little post-modern uniform dress by Miuccia Prada that I picked up. I went just the teensiest bit over my credit limit."

Daddy tousled my hair, which I just hate. As a display of affection, it works better with golden retrievers.

My cell phone, which had been ringing regularly since the first airing of the tape, interrupted our heart-to-heart. "Whoops," I said, ducking out from under the parental palm. "I'd better get that—although I can't think of anyone who hasn't already checked in."

It was true. All my buds had called, and since I am

one of the most popular Bettys at Bronson Alcott High, that meant that I'd barely had time to toss down a nonfat yogurt all day. I was ravenous. "Lucy," I called to our housekeeper while clicking on my mobile, "could you nuke a batch of popcorn for me, please?"

In the crisp white uniform I'd handpicked for her and these dire black orthopedic shoes she'd treated herself to, Lucy peeked out of the den. "I can't. I'm busy," she said.

"What are you doing?"

"Watching Bob Saget. I love that show."

"Well, do it during the commercial, okay?"

She disappeared into the den again, grumbling, "What am I, your maid?"

"Well, technically, yes," I called, but she was gone and my protégée, Tai, was on the line. De and I had done a chronic makeover on her, but the girl was basically naive and a total magnet for slackers and geeks.

"I hope I'm not bothering you, Cher, but I forgot to tell you this other thing," she said excitedly. "Remember I said I saw you guys on the closed-caption TV at Caffeine Café, that place where they serve only Colombian coffee? Well, guess who else was there?"

I walked into the kitchen. "If it was some guy in white pajamas and a colorful serape, I think they call him Juan Valdés," I said, checking out the cabinet for microwavable popcorn, although I knew air-popped was the healthier choice.

"Duh, like I wouldn't recognize Juan Valdés from the commercial?" Tai replied. "As if. No, Cher, it was this adorable new guy from Italy who's starting school tomorrow. He said he already met you—"

"Aldo?" The bag of grease-saturated taco chips I'd unconsciously grabbed fell from my hands. It was like this little fitness miracle.

"That's him," Tai confirmed. "He was sitting right next to me, having a cappuccino, when the news came on."

"Was he alone?" I asked.

"Way past that," she said. "He looked terminally friendless. I'd say bordering on depressed—that is, until your face showed up on the set over the espresso machine. Then he cheered up majorly. So then I said, 'I know that girl.' And he goes, 'Me too,' or something like that but with this classic accent. He was really glad to see you."

"Then what happened?" I pressed.

"Oh, well, then my friend Ryder—you know, the one who like grosses everyone out with his food tricks—he came back from the bathroom and he wouldn't take off his skates, so they made us leave—"

"No, no, I mean did Aldo say anything about me?"

"Just some Italian stuff. He seemed very nice, but Ryder and I thought maybe we'd like catch a ride to Venice. Only the bus driver said Ryder couldn't get on with skates, and he got all bent out of shape—"

"Thanks, Tai. I need some time alone now to contemplate ensemble choices. See you tomorrow," I said, and clicked off.

On my way up our graciously curved white-carpeted

staircase, I speed-dialed Dionne. "Never mind, Lucy," I called over the banister as De's mobile began to ring. "I'm starting a diet anyway." Finally, as I entered my palest pink Laura Ashley–papered room, Dionne picked up. There was a booming rap beat behind her cheery hello that told me Murray was near.

"Guess who saw me on TV?" I said.

"Girlfriend, you don't expect me to recite the Beverly Hills directory name by name, do you?"

"Aldo Belloguardia!" I shouted.

"Murray, Murray, the new Baldwin I told you about caught Cher's small-screen debut! I don't believe it. No way!" De exploded with delight.

"Way, girlfriend! Majorly way!" I assured her.

"I'm totally kvelling," said Dionne. "How'd you find out? Did he call you?"

"Tai delivered the bulletin cellularly. So now of course I'm all ensembly indecisive." The pounding bass background noise was heinous. I had to holler every word. "How am I going to greet the boy tomorrow? I've got my new Miuccia, but it's kind of severe, and the Versace is too viciously festive. De, it's four P.M. on a Sunday afternoon. Like what professional hair person would even plug in a blow-dryer on such short notice? I'm probably going to have to style it myself."

"Always risky," De agreed.

"Talk me through this, Dionne," I urged. "I'm seriously hyperventilating. Where are you?"

"Murray is exercising his option to drive. Like having a license makes it absolutely mandatory to cruise a freeway, with every lapsed learner's permit in L.A.

tearing by. It's this macho initiation rite. I can hardly hear you—"

"Well, duh, ask Murray to turn down the CD player. That music reeks anyway."

"It's not us," De shouted. "The loqued-out Jeep two lanes to the left is providing the sounds. Just shout."

Much as I needed support, I didn't feel I could project at that level any longer. "Call me later!" I yelled, and clicked off.

And then, the way it always seems to happen for me, at my creative ebb, inspiration struck. I realized I could do a hands-across-the-sea type of look. Rather than try to match Aldo's def Continental aura, I'd go totally American.

My walk-in closet was teeming with Kleins (Anne and Calvin), Ralph, Tommy, Donna K, and more. I might even go with something radically mall from Eddie Bauer, Victoria's Secret, Express, or the Gap. At least I had a concept to work with. It made me feel extremely better. I phoned the den. Lucy picked up. "If it's not too much trouble, Luce," I said, "I'd like an indigenous dinner—but low-cal. Let's go in the turkey-burger direction. With basic American condiments."

"Right after *Lois and Clark*," she promised.

Chapter 4

Monday morning I did a white linen, blue T-shirt, strappy red sandals thing, which I topped off with an adorable floppy-brimmed straw hat, beneath which my highlighted hair silkenly cascaded. Trekking cross-campus, I could tell I'd scored another victory. Fashion enthusiasts greeted me with wide-eyed awe and unanimous thumbs-up. A few even saluted, which I found excessive.

I whirled for Murray and De, who were engaged in their ritual debate at our regular table in the Quad. They must have begun the argument du jour moments before my arrival, because the usual fight fans hadn't gathered yet.

"For your information, Dionne," Murray was saying, pointing at her with two fingers, "my apparel choices connote an allegiance to my community rather than

slavish observance of bourgeois costume conventions."
He was wearing a red, green, and black running suit, a
checkered golf cap pulled low on his brow, several rings,
and a medallion that looked like Dunkin' Donuts was
having a sale on gold-dipped crullers.

"Hel*lo!*" I coughed to get their attention. And was
furiously ignored.

"My ensemble is merely emblematic," Murray asserted.

De rolled her eyes. "All that ensemble is emblematic
of, Murray, is your couch-potato status. You've obviously been zoning on gangsta rap videos again."

"*Ding, ding!* End of round one," I announced. They
totally didn't hear me.

Jesse, Sean, and Morrissey had strolled over to the
table. "Perhaps, you'd like a little downtime to reevalu-
ate my point of view," Murray said, slapping high fives
all around.

"Starting yesterday!" De responded. Then she finally
saw me, and her frown gave way to a monster smile.
"Classic linen look," she said. "With a clever hint of
patriotic verve. Bye, Murray. We're Audi."

"Catch you later," Murray called after her as we
headed off to class.

We ran into Amber in the corridor outside Mr. Hall's
room. She made a big thing of looking me over. "Excuse
me, is it like the Fourth of July only I forgot and went to
summer school?" she said.

Amber herself was clothed in a crop-top hip-hugger
pants suit that seemed to be made of the same white
pearlized plastic stuff that gift baskets of fruit jellies

come wrapped in. I chose not to comment on her outfit. First because she *is* a friend. But more importantly because a rebuff from Amber is often a very valuable envy indicator. So I was way pleased.

De bailed for Hanratty's math, and Amber, her plastic suit swishing audibly with every step, followed me into Hall's classroom.

A blinding light from the fourth seat, third row, signaled the Baldwinian presence of Aldo Belloguardia. I found myself drawn to him the way weirdos who buy into the UFO thing go all awestruck at unexplained lights in the sky. It was his adorable grin, the welcoming sparkle in his eyes as they beheld me, and, of course, the clean, unstuffy Helmut Lang suit he was wearing with his excellent stretch nylon polo shirt. Also there was the superfine coincidence that my seat was practically next to his.

"Buon giorno," he said softly as I moved up the aisle. "I see you on TV. You are a hero, no? Cher"—he pronounced it "Chair," which I have to say sounded frantically lyrical—"you are no just beautiful but also . . . how you say, *coraggiosa."*

"Courageous," Baez, whose mom was once married to an Italian pop star, translated for us. She was sitting in front of Aldo. She swiveled to face him now. "Didn't you nearly bug when you saw her?" she said. "I mean, I was all channel-surfing, and suddenly there's Cher going on about this mall outlaw."

"Yes, I do," he said, dark eyes laughing. "I bug when I see her."

I could feel myself starting to blush. Which is so not me! After the time I'd put in perfecting my appearance, having my pigments in an uproar was way jarring.

I tried to shrug it off. "What else was there to do? I mean the man could have been incarcerated for his clothing choices alone," I said, slipping into my seat. "It's so jammin' to catch you in Mr. Hall's class, Aldo," I confided. "He's a totally righteous teacher, way supportive about most things but not entirely flexible on negotiating grades."

Mr. Hall overheard me. "Thank you, Cher." He did this cute little bow, then sneezed. The two strands of hair that crossed his balding crown flopped forward, and he raked them back good-naturedly. On top of follicle fallout and shortness of stature, Mr. Hall is sometimes plagued by hay fever. "And welcome . . ." Sniffling, he glanced at the attendance card on his desk. "Er, Mr. Belloguardia," he said. "Aldo, is it?"

Aldo did this little nod and shy smile. And like half the class went, "Oooooh, Aldo." And "Baldwin alert." And "Awesome." Behind me, Janet Hong whispered, "I'm totally plotzing."

"Settle down, class," said Mr. Hall. "Okay, earphones out, CD players off. Let's put away our blow-dryers and cosmetics, everyone. Ryder, what are you doing?"

"Swabbing my navel ring, Mr. Hall. The dude who performed the piercing said I have to clean off the crud every half hour or else it'll—"

"No details, please. Thank you, Ryder," said Mr. Hall. "Paroudasm," he called on the prince of the Iranian

27

posse, who was ranting to his crew at the back of the room. "Would you care to share that with the whole class?"

Parou stood up among his snickering subjects and let loose a stream of way harsh Farsi.

"In English please, Mr. Banafshein," Hall prompted.

"I was just saying that if he had gotten real gold there would be no cause for alarm. It is only cheap imitation—"

"I don't wear real gold." Ryder stood up, pointing severely at Paroudasm. "Unlike some people who have like totally no conscience about what happens to our planet! I mean, once we use up all the gold, it's like gone, man. But what do you care about that, right? As long as you've got your Rolex and earring and chains, man."

There was a smattering of applause, a couple of groans, and a sneeze from Mr. Hall. Also, there were some choice phrases in Farsi, Spanish, and Japanese. But no Italian. Aldo was quietly taking it all in.

"Thank you for that impassioned explanation," Mr. Hall said. "Ryder, Paroudasm, be seated, please. Now, class, as you know I am the faculty adviser for our school newspaper, the *Bronson Alcott Buzz*—"

"You mean the Bzzzzzzz?" Ryder did his annoying insect impersonation.

"The Bronson Alcott what?" Sean asked.

"*Buzz*," Mr. Hall repeated.

"Okay. Buzzzzzzzzzz." Kids were buzzing and doing bee imitations all over the room.

"Okay, I get it. I say *Buzz*. You buzz. Very entertaining," said Mr. Hall. "Well, we certainly got a lot of participation on that. Let's talk about participation for a moment. Traditionally, the next edition of the, er, school paper is entirely created by your class. So today I'm looking for representatives to work on it. To contribute articles, poems, essays, what have you. Any volunteers? Anyone interested?"

The mass silence was interrupted only by a beeper going off and all the kids checking to see if it was theirs. "I got it. It's my broker. No huge deal," Jesse announced. "Go ahead, Mr. Hall."

"Why, thank you, Jesse," Hall said. Then he looked over the class, and his little pollen-inflamed eyes settled pinkly on me. "Cher, how about you? We need someone to head up our effort, to be our chief correspondent. I know you've contributed to the, er, newspaper in the past. From what I've heard, your powers of observation were put to a very practical test this weekend."

His remarks were greeted by cheers, cries of "You go, girl," and a burst of desk- and floor-stomping. I stood for the ovation and thanked my supporters.

"And," Mr. Hall shouted, bringing the demonstration to a close, "Cher, I think heading up our class effort would help you further develop that skill, as well as your striking descriptive flair. Your remarks about the mall purse-snatcher were certainly vivid. And the videotape that you and Dionne made—"

"Hello! I think I'm entitled to a credit here." Amber leaped to her feet. "It was my camera!"

"Sorry, Amber," Mr. Hall said consolingly. "Does this mean that you'd like to work on the *Buzz?*"

"The what?" Paroudasm called, and half the class started buzzing again, and the other half groaned.

"As if." With a crackle of pearlized plastic, Amber took her seat.

"Cher, I think you'd be a valuable member of our staff. What do you say?"

I knew why Mr. Hall was singling me out. My leadership skills are way honed. I'm like a born CEO. And not just in life's cosmetic and couture departments. If I signed on, others would follow. So I wanted to give his invite serious consideration. I glanced over at Aldo. His dark-eyed gaze had strayed from me. He was staring out the classroom window, his classic brow crumpled in worried concentration.

Turning from Aldo inward, I considered Mr. Hall's needs. Although I was in solid accord with his appraisal of my talents, working on the *Alcott Buzz* would involve even more writing than I was currently committed to. I thought of the book reports, term papers, and magazine questionnaires I already had on my plate. To say nothing of weight training and aerobics, tennis, tanning, and the many other nonliterary electives in my life. I was way overbooked.

"Surely someone will volunteer," Mr. Hall said.

To my amazement, Aldo's hand went up. My heart totally leaped. Not only was the boy a brutal Baldwin, but he was a mature, socially responsible hottie as well. He was going to volunteer for the paper. The least I could do was support his activism.

I sprang to my feet. "All right, Mr. Hall," I said. "I accept your challenge. I'll work on the *Buzz*."

"Good. Yes, Aldo?"

"*Scusi.* I mean, you excuse me, Mr. Hall, but I have urgent business. I must go now. Um, I go to see my counselor . . . er, how you say, the gwee-dance—"

"Guidance," Baez suggested helpfully.

"You mean your guidance counselor?" I asked.

"*Sì,* yes. The counselor." He threw me a grateful nod and began gathering up his books. "Later I explain, please. Is very, very important."

"But, Aldo, I thought you were going to join the newspaper," I blurted.

He did this poignant palms-up shrug and threw me a modest grin. "No with my English. But you, Cher. Again I see your courage. And I, how to say . . . I admire, yes. Very much. I am . . . proud to you." And with this meltingly sweet, almost apologetic glance at me, he rushed from the room.

I was taken aback. Which is majorly rare. But I had so not expected him to abscond.

"All right, class." Mr. Hall wriggled his nose against the itch of hay fever. "Cher has led the way. Would anyone else like to join?"

"Mr. Hall," I started to say as his sneeze erupted, "actually I'm like reconsidering my decision—"

But he'd already called on Janet, who was avidly waving her hand and going, "Mr. Hall, Mr. Hall. I've got this extremely prime idea for a story Cher could do! Because she's so cutting edge on the accessory front."

Feeling thwarted and perplexed, I glanced out the window—and there was Aldo! He was hurrying across the grassy slope of the Quad, heading toward an enormous black limousine that was idling at the curb.

Standing beside the silver-windowed stretch was a tall, dark cigar smoker. Although he was some distance away, the man's suit cried out Armani. His sunglasses said Mossimo. Nothing about him even murmured guidance counselor.

I speed-dialed Dionne. "Are you in algebra?" I whispered, while Janet outlined this lame yet arduous reporting assignment for me. "Girlfriend, something totally *X-Files* is going on."

In hushed tones I detailed for De how Mr. Hall had been doing this recruitment drive for the *Buzz* when suddenly Aldo had gotten all agitated, concocted the guidance-counselor ruse, and bailed. "It's okay if he's not into the Clark Kent thing," I told her, "but his reaction was way extreme. Plus like a minute later he's outside, rushing toward this dark, distinguished stranger draped in excellent Armani threads. Look out the window. Can you see him?"

"Yes," De said, "but you're off about the suit. It's Gucci. And the so hip yet comfortable soft neutral suede loafers are one hundred percent Granello."

"Whatever," I said. "But I think you'll agree, Dionne, the man doesn't look anything like a guidance counselor."

"Not even if he wore a pocket protector," she confirmed. There was a moment of silence as, from our separate classrooms, De and I watched the designer-clad mystery man greeting Aldo. The stranger hugged him, then held him at arm's length and clamped Aldo's golden face between his hands.

"Cher." It was Mr. Hall. I shoved the cell phone under my desk and smiled brightly at him.

"Is there any reason you wouldn't consider Janet's story suggestion on the illegal imitation designer scarves and watches flooding the American marketplace?"

"You mean aside from the fact that it would take about a year to research?" I said.

"How about doing an exposé of cafeteria cutbacks?" Annabell suggested. "I hear they're using faux mesclun for the salads, and the supposedly low-cal goat cheese is actually reconstituted Velveeta."

" 'Reconstituted' is redundant," Janet pointed out.

"Whatever," Amber said, coming to Annabell's defense.

Then Ryder jumped into the discussion, taking an impassioned stand for Velveeta, Kraft slices, and processed cheese in general. I got back on the horn with De.

"Quick, look," she said.

I peered out the window just in time to see the Gucci man disappear into the backseat of the car. Aldo followed him, the rear door slammed shut, and the sleek black limo sped away.

"Was that not furiously enigmatic?" I remarked.

"Way strange," De agreed. Then she went "Whoops!" and clicked off.

Which was so whack. Because at my vulnerable low, while I was still addled by Aldo's disappearing act and reeling from De's abrupt disconnect, Mr. Hall finally called on me.

"Well, class," he said first, "we'll have our editorial staff meeting tomorrow, Tuesday, at twelve-thirty, right here. I suggest that each of you write down your stimulating suggestions for *Buzz* articles and submit them to our new chief correspondent, Cher! I think she'll do us proud."

Proud. Aldo had said that, too.

As my peers applauded, whistled, stamped, and tossed crumpled paper at one another, I recalled the precious last words Aldo had uttered to me before he bailed out of class: "I am . . . proud to you."

"Cher, you had your hand up?" Mr. Hall said.

"Never mind," I replied.

Chapter 5

*T*he morning had fled as swiftly as the mall felon. I didn't catch up with Dionne again until our lunch break. Amber, Tai, and I ran into her as she emerged from the administration office, looking hugely cranky.

"Whoops?" I said, greeting her with a limp-wristed high five. "Girlfriend, I've been puzzling over that communication since you severed me during first period."

Tai and Amber pushed open the bronze doors at the end of the corridor, and the four of us burst from the dim recesses of the building into a glaring smog alert. Murmurs of "I love your outfit" and "Where did you get your mood ring?" and "Do you want to copy my homework?" accompanied us as we strode down the front steps. We were just a quartet of popular Bettys on our way to the cafeteria patio for a grilled salmon and Portabello mushroom fest. Hardly anyone noticed Dionne's dark mood. Including Tai.

"Is your phone broken?" she innocently asked De. "I tried you twice this morning. Once from science when we took a break from frog-hacking while Summer did this rant on the sacredness of all living things. Then once from the pool. Alana was brutally bummed because Ms. Stoeger made her go swimming despite the note from the salesman at Speedo about how overchlorination could destroy the elasticity of her new racing suit—"

"Loosely translated," Dionne said coldly, " 'whoops' was my way of saying, 'I'm toast.' Mrs. Hanratty is breathing denture breath down my neck. She's standing right here with her liver-spotted hand out, demanding my Motorola!"

Actually, Hanratty's teeth were too flawed to be faux, or else she'd been brutally played by her dentist; and while her paws were so not acquainted with serious alpha-hydroxy moisturizers, they were not yet fully decrepit. So I knew my best friend was in pain.

"You mean she took your phone away!" Amber was horrified. "What is she like campaigning for most insensitive teacher of the year?"

"De, forgive me," I urged. "I didn't know."

"I have been phoneless for four hours, Cher! I was viciously hyperventilating."

I took her arm; I patted her hand. "It's all right. You're safe now," I whispered. "You're with us."

"Is that why you were in the office?" Tai asked. "To see the nurse?"

"I was in the office for a mandatory chat with Mr. Lehman, our principal." De was bitterly stressed. "Who almost didn't give me back my cellular. Like I had to vow not to use it during class!"

"That so blows," said Amber.

De sighed heavily. "It was pretty touch and go," she admitted.

"Guess what happened to Cher?" said Tai.

Dionne's deeply concerned hazel eyes scanned my face. "Oh, no, girlfriend. Was your cellular seized as well?"

"Nothing that brutal. Still, it's no bed of roses. I'm the new chief correspondent to the *Alcott Buzz*."

"The what?" Tai said, giggling.

I threw her a silencing look and tossed my backpack onto our reserved table.

"I think it's a total sham how teachers get reserved parking and students have to like wait for valet," Jesse Fiegenhut, who was holding a tray of mineral water and sun-dried tomato ravioli, called out to me. "Make them see the truth, Cher!"

"Right arm!" Ryder skated by, thrusting a leather-gloved fist in the air.

De and I crashed at the table while Tai and Amber hit the cafeteria to scope out luncheon choices.

"You would not believe what they were doing to frogs in Mr. Latimer's class!" Summer dropped her biology text on the table. "I'm going to get a veggie burger,

Cher. Then I want to talk to you about an important issue I think you should write up for the *Buzz*."

"Just a wild guess, but is like amphibian abuse involved?" I asked.

"That is so cynical," Summer said. "I'll be right back."

De grinned at me. "Congratulations. Chief correspondent looks like a brutally popular post."

"Condolences are more like it. De, it's lonely at the top. But you know what would be radically down? Like why don't you join up too. I mean, this is a superfine op to speak out against cellular snatching and any other grievances you want to air."

"Tempting," De agreed. "So what happened after I hung up? Was there a break in the Aldo story? Have you seen the sizzler since his chauffeured abduction?"

"I don't know his full Monday schedule, but I haven't seen him since the limo episode," I replied as Murray and Jared pulled up to the table.

"'Sup, woman? What's dope on the carte today?" Murray snagged a seat next to De. I could sense her stiffening at the *W*-word.

"He's baiting you." I put a gently restraining French-manicured hand on her arm. "He's just a high school boy, Dionne, even if he has got his driver's license. He can't help it. Just don't respond." It was too late.

"'Woman'?" she huffed. "How many times do I have to tell you how demeaning I find it to be referred to generically?"

"And I am supposed to alleviate your discomfort in what way?" Murray wanted to know.

"One," said De, holding up a pale juliette. "You could apologize—"

"Yo, yo, yo! Chill, woman. You know I can't be doin' that." Murray placed a hand on his heart. "You talkin' to a man here. Real men don't be sayin' they're sorry—"

"I'm Audi," Jared said, and bailed.

De and Murray tend to recycle familiar themes. Sometimes they focus on an actual issue that plagues them. Then their discussions become truly vibrant. Too often, however, they dwell on ancient complaints. Which keeps their debating skills honed and attracts a good crowd but can be a brutal yawn if you've known them practically forever.

While I waited for a lull in the proceedings, I got this stroke of brilliance. "Excuse me. Hello. May I have your attention?" I said as De paused for breath. "If you've got a lemon, make lemonade, girlfriend."

She turned toward me, momentarily receptive.

"Dionne, I have this excellent idea. Why not turn your feelings on this issue into a crusading Op-Ed piece for the *Buzz?* An article on how communication between the sexes influences relationships—you know, like 'Men Are from Mars and Boys Are from' . . . some totally other place," I improvised. "Just think about it, okay? And, Murray, you can do a viciously articulate rebuff in the same edition. Catch you later," I said. "I'm going to get a tray and check out today's low-cal options."

"Pick me up a spinach salad," De said. "No bacon bits, egg crumbs, or croutons—unless they're baked, not fried."

I had barely downloaded my brainstorm on De and

Murray when my mind clicked onto Aldo again. I hadn't realized how stressed I was by his strange behavior until I sauntered into the cafeteria and found myself drawn to the junk-food end of the grill. Hamburgers reeking of charred fat and hot dogs plump with unknowable fillers called to me for a moment.

Shaken, I turned away. Tai and Amber were studying desserts at the gourmet end of the steam tables. I hurried to them. "I almost bowed to a burger," I confessed.

Amber put her arm around my shoulders. Her pearl-ized sleeve felt oddly soothing. "Think bovine," she whispered. "Cows in, cows out. It's simple."

"That is so wise," I replied, grateful for her wisdom.

"Try the pasta," Tai encouraged. "It's extremely meatless."

"I think I'll stick with greens today. Pasta is such a carbo load. Plus I'm feeling way too vulnerable for anything Italian."

"Is it Aldo? I saw the sparks between you two today . . . and then it was so weird the way he ran out of class," Amber said, passing me a salad.

I picked up another one for De and began to pick out the little fried croutons which so few people understand can turn an innocent salad into a minefield of hidden fat.

"Cher, Cher, yo, girl, listen up." Sean was suddenly beside us, all breathless and beaming. "I got this chronic notion for a sounds column you could do. You know a kind of 'Ask the Rap Bandit,' 'Bobbito Plays the Tracks,'

40

Vibe type of Q-and-A on assorted eclectic yet racially aware themes for men—"

"Props, Sean." I paused with a greasy little crouton in my fingers. "You could call it Boyz R Us."

"Phat. So you'll do it."

"Not even. It's your concept—"

"Yeah, but you're chief correspondent," he said indignantly. "Know what? I'm sorry I even voted for you." He turned the brim of his Kangol cap to one side and stalked off to the latte bar.

"Excuse me. Reality check. You didn't," I called after him. "I volunteered."

"Sean can be shallow," Tai commiserated, "although I'm basically a fan of his. But like why did you volunteer?"

"That's a good question, Tai." She picked up a chocolate nut brownie, and Amber selected the mango mousse, and we carried our trays toward the cashier's line. "Actually, I felt sure that Aldo wanted to work on the paper, and I merely planned to support his effort."

"Then he brutally bailed on you, and you were stuck," Amber added.

"And then I realized," I corrected her, "that not just Aldo but all of my classmates needed me. I am an excellent writer, and I would be even if I didn't have SpellCheck on my Mac. And as Mr. Hall pointed out, I've already had a successful journalistic-type experience— describing and helping to apprehend the mall criminal."

We moved into the express line. "Charge it to my account," I told the cashier, then signed the receipt.

"But I'm only one person," I said to Amber and Tai. "And I would very much appreciate a little help here."

"What, like you want us to join the newspaper too?" Tai guessed. "I don't know, Cher. I'm not that good a writer."

"Well, I am," Amber crowed. "I mean, grades are not a fair evaluation of talent. They're just one person's opinion. And an underpaid person at that."

We evacuated the stuffy cafeteria and elbowed our way through the lunchtime throng on the patio. De waved as we approached the table. Murray had gone.

"Murray and I talked over your idea about the gender articles," she said, sliding her spinach salad off the tray. "We're both psyched. And we both want to work on the *Buzz* with you, okay?"

"Excellent," I said. "Amber? Tai?"

"Well, I'll try," Tai murmured tentatively.

We all looked at Amber.

"Only if you'll go to the Surgical Enhancement Imaging Institute with me after school," she said.

"Yeeeuuww!" we shrieked.

"No way," Dionne said. "Last time they had these books full of before-and-after pics of like liposuction and skin-peel candidates. Remember, Cher?"

"Ugh," I groaned. "It was cellulite city in raging Technicolor!"

"Let's be realistic, Cher." Amber confidently flipped back her hair. "I want to check out the latest enhancement procedures. You want my support for your new journalistic endeavor. Is compromise a possibility?"

"Hey, maybe that imaging place would make a good

story," Tai said with a burst of enthusiasm. "I mean, how many kids in this entire school even remember their first noses? Let alone their original parents?"

"Out of the mouths of babes," De said. "Cher, I think Tai's onto a solid scenario. We could take care of Amber's companionship needs and do like a research jaunt for the paper at the same time."

"This is so amazing." Amber was aglow with revelation. "I bet if we tell the institute that we're going to do a story about them, they'll like give us a discount."

"On what?" Tai asked.

"Whatever." Amber got annoyed. "Brow lift, lip poufing . . . we're not going to be young, popular, and perfect forever. I am so glad I thought of it."

"You didn't," De pointed out. "It was Tai's idea."

"Excuse me?" Amber pointed a white juliette at Dionne. "Tai would not even have had the idea if I hadn't brought up the institute in the first place. And anyway I meant the discount. Which is the totally most golden idea I've had all day."

"I thought wrapping yourself as a gift basket was kind of interesting," De commented.

Amber ignored her. "So you're all coming with me, right?"

"I can't." Tai's hands were resting in her lap. She looked down at them. "I'm grounded."

"Why?" I asked.

"For skating with Ryder—"

"That's a way harsh punishment for just having bad taste in boys," De blurted sympathetically.

"—in the house," Tai finished. "He was like skating

down the banister when Mom walked in"—she shook her head—"carrying this antique vase my grandmother got for a wedding present that had just been repaired because I'd accidentally chipped it the week before when Eric Fosbo was teaching me how to jump into a mosh pit."

"Eric Fosbo? What a loser," Amber remarked. "The one who wears safety pins?"

"Not everyone can afford gold lip rings." Tai defended the drooling slacker. "Anyway, I'm way despondent, but I can't make it this afternoon."

"That's okay," Amber assured her. "You can make it up to me some other way." Then she turned to De and me. "But you're on, right?"

"And you're writing the story for the *Buzz?*" I said.

"Totally," she agreed, "and snagging the discount, too!"

Which is why, at four that afternoon, De and I found ourselves sitting in the over-air-conditioned waiting room of the Surgical Enhancement Imaging Institute. Amber had demanded to see the director, and this platinum-coiffed receptionist, who looked like Tori Spelling garbed by Uniforms 4-US, whisked her away.

The waiting room was heavy on mirrors. Which was a clever way to drum up business, I thought. I mean, if you're stuck staring at wraparound reflections of yourself long enough, you're bound to spot some body part that could benefit from a snip, stitch, lift, or tuck. And they had brochures all over the place that showed you how they'd do it. Which, on the taste scale, went from beyond not necessary to full-out gross. And, of course, glowing like toxic waste on the mirrored coffee tables were the massive before-and-after scrapbooks De and I had once made the mistake of browsing.

This sleazy soft music was pumped in to help relax you or something. But it was way annoying. Like having to go to Burt Bacharach at the Hollywood Bowl with your grandparents.

I found the entire environment extremely manipulative. They did everything but suction the credit cards out of your wallet. Anyway, I was Audi—all up in my head, cruising Aldo Land—when De called me home.

"So like what raving exposé do you have in mind, girlfriend? Hel*lo!* Earth to Cher."

"I was just thinking," I said.

"Of what? Wait, let me guess. Was it cappuccino, Ferragamo, ravioli, or Belloguardia?"

"The latter," I confessed. "Although a decent cup of Italian roast would be way welcome. It's fully freezing in here."

"Did you see him this afternoon?"

"No, why?" I said, elated with hope. "Was he back at school?"

Dionne shrugged. "I didn't see him. I just wondered if he'd returned. So what I was saying, girlfriend, is like Murray and I are going to do the language-and-gender article. And Amber is committed to the surgical-enhancement piece. Do you have a story in mind?"

"Who do you think the guy with the cigar was?" I asked.

De scanned the waiting room. There were three people there besides us: two women and a man with a bandaged nose. All of them were wearing these fashion-ably huge sun shades, although the room was totally dim. It took De a moment to catch up with me. "Oh, you mean the stretch-limo guy? Maybe he was Aldo's chauffeur?"

I shook my head. "No. I mean, even if Italian limo drivers dress better than ours, I just didn't get a service-industry vibe from him. The man had this like regal bearing."

"Plus"—De did a quick revise—"unless he'd been with the family forever, I think his greeting betrayed a more intimate relationship."

"Or," I hypothesized, "a more sinister one."

"Like what? I mean, Aldo wasn't kidnapped or any-thing. You said he got up and left on his own."

"That's true. But it wasn't like he wanted to go. It was more like he had to or—"

"Or what?" De asked.

"I don't know. I hope Aldo's not mixed up in anything dangerous."

"Dangerous?" Amber swished across the waiting room to us. She looked very pleased with herself. "There's nothing dangerous in this entire place. They're furiously certified," she asserted, studying her spiral-bound notepad.

"We weren't talking about the perils of rhino-plasty—" I began.

"It's all here." Ignoring my interruption, she tapped the notepad with her pen. "The Surgical Enhancement Imaging Institute is one of the most advanced facilities of its kind with a wide variety of pre- and postoperative cosmetic services and designs."

Without pausing for air, Amber sat down opposite us. "The director and I had a very fruitful heart-to-heart, and I have to say I'm delighted with the package I negotiated. Okay, I get a totally free complimentary computer-imaging session, and you two get to watch how it's done. Is that awesome?"

"Less than," De said.

"Well, I did my best, and he drove a very hard bargain, and I'm not going to break out in hives over your attitude, Dionne. The computer technician is going to call us soon. So you weren't talking about my article?"

"No, we were trying to figure out why Aldo skipped so abruptly today. Cher thinks he might be in trouble."

"That's just one of an infinite number of possibilities," I corrected Dionne. "He seemed kind of disturbed when he left class, and there was this big black limo waiting outside, and a tall excellently clad man—"

"What if he's like a movie star?" De guessed. "Aldo, not the guy who hugged him. I mean, maybe the man was his agent. They hug people a lot, and they dress way better than the stars, usually."

"What, like Aldo's a movie star and we—devout readers of *Sassy, Seventeen, YM, Teen,* and *Elle,* to say nothing of *W, Vogue, Details,* and *People*—we'd really have not heard of him? I don't think so," Amber said.

"In Italy, not here," De explained. "Maybe he's an Italian movie star or like major television personality—"

"A soap stud," Amber suggested.

"And he's in Los Angeles to make an American movie. That is so possible," I said. "I mean, the boy is a brutal hunk—"

"A moment, please." Amber held up a pause finger. "Are they going to like dub the whole movie? Aldo's a blazing Baldwin, true, but his English-language skills reek."

Our discussion was tabled when the Tori look-alike signaled us. "Dr. Kharkomoun will see you now," she said, pointing the way. "Third door on your left." A shiver of excitement went through me as we headed toward the computer-imaging area. Or maybe I was just chilled to the bone from waiting in the mirrored Freon pit.

Behind door number three, we spent an amusing hour watching Amber try on the latest in facial enhancements. She swished and crinkled her pearlized self into a chair in front of a TV-size computer with a camera mounted on top of it.

Dr. K. fixed Amber's image on the monitor and, after a short discussion of options, set to work. With a wand, she touched and prodded the screen, plumping a lip here, removing some chin there, pinning back a wayward ear.

"What's brachioplasty?" De asked, looking at the makeover menu we'd been handed.

"You might want to check with Murray," I said, "but I think it's when you get your brachs lubed."

Amber fiercely cut her eyes at us. "That is so not funny," she said. "Tell her, Dr. K."

"Brachioplasty is a surgical procedure to lift and tighten the upper-arm skin," the doctor said.

"It's about flab," Amber ranted, "which can so alter a person's self-image. I mean, imagine a life without sleeveless options."

"Dire," I agreed.

"I'm brutally bored," said De.

"I think we're finished here," Dr. K. said. "What do you think, Amber?"

Amber studied her renovated image on the computer screen. "It's so subtle," she said. "I mean, I can hardly notice the difference."

The doctor returned her wand to its holder and pushed a button, and out popped a souvenir before-and-after Polaroid to take home. On the right side was the original image of Amber; on the left was Cameron Diaz.

Chapter 6

*T*uesday morning dawned so clean that I broke out my new ivory rayon dress with plunging V neck by Ozbek and tied my lustrous highlighted hair into a casually wispy ponytail.

Daddy was in the kitchen bolting down his breakfast. I caught him stuffing the last piece of a treacherous artery-clogging croissant into his mouth. He looked so adorably guilty.

"You're not going to school dressed like that." It was a transparent diversion to mask his shame. Plus it told me that my ensemble was a rave. "You march right upstairs this minute, young lady, and change into normal school clothes," he ordered, furiously blotting the telltale crumbs from his lips with a Calvin Klein linen napkin.

"Normal? Since when is that the standard in this house?" I asked him.

"March," he insisted.

"But, Daddy, you've always said I should strive for excellence, and this is the most excellent new dress in my collection."

He relented. "Well, put something on over it."

"Yes, Daddy," I said on my way out. "And don't think I didn't see you stuffing that fatty embolism into your system."

The morning's promise was fully kept when I arrived at school. I was doing a solo on a warm, sun-drenched bench near the steps. The fresh Betsey Johnson cotton sweater I'd grabbed was lying beside me. The mochaccino I'd ordered was golden. The shrubbery provided a fragrant backdrop of freesia and hibiscus blooms.

I was quietly reviewing my homework, comparing it with the answers Ringo Farbstein, the mathmeister, had given me, when a way welcome voice called my name. Or the Italian equivalent of it.

"Chair," I heard.

I looked up. Sunlight framed his sleek golden head and silhouetted his glorious Baldwin bod. I propped up my Web shades.

"Aldo?"

"*Buon giorno. Come stai?* How you are?" He'd lost the jacket but was wearing a creamy cashmere V neck over a noble Mediterranean-blue button-down. Linen pants by Hugo Boss. And what was that gleaming in his right ear—a stylishly petite gold ring?

"I'm way decent. And so is that accessory. Did you get it yesterday?" I probed. "I mean, did you like go shopping—"

"Oh, no." The boy reddened velvetly. "No, no. Yesterday, I . . . No. So you like the earring?" He toyed with his earlobe. "It's good, no? And I like you . . ." He surveyed me head to toe, then laughed suddenly. "I like you everything," he said.

I opted to accept the compliment with a silent but solid smile. Then the bell rang, startling us both. "So what's your first class?" I asked.

He checked his notebook. "Algebra. *Con . . . Scusi.* I mean, with . . . Ann Ratty."

"Mrs. Ratty? Oh," I said. "Duh." I struck my forehead—but lightly. "You mean, Mrs. Hanratty. I've got her for third period. Want me to show you where it is?"

"*Sì.* Yes. Please. But I must carry your books, no?"

"Not even," I said. "I'll just stuff them in here." I put my homework, Ringo's notes, and my classic sweater into my backpack and slung it over my shoulder. Then Aldo and I strolled up the school steps, besieged by glances and greetings.

We paused in the hall outside Hanratty's algebra class. Aldo thanked me profusely for walking him to the door and suggested we meet for lunch. I checked his schedule card and said, "Doable. Twelve-thirty on the patio. Ask for my table." Then we said ciao and parted.

My instinct was to contact De. Like instantly. But I remembered that she was hobbled by the ban on cellular communication. So I speed-dialed Amber, who had social studies with her.

"Amber on the line," she said by way of greeting.

"Hey, girlfriend. Was that you in the iridescent pea-green boot pants this A.M.?" I asked.

"Yes. From Todd Oldham's spring collection, previewed in French *Vogue*. Who is this?"

"Amber, it's Cher," I replied impatiently.

"Well, not everyone who calls me is you," she said. "I've been getting compliments on my ensemble all morning. Being a trendsetter is way exhausting."

I caught a glimpse of Mr. Hall struggling against the tides of corridor chaos. In threadbare khakis, a faded blue oxford, and an ancient knit tie in like maroon, which is not even a color anymore. He looked so adorably teacherly. He had a pencil gripped in his teeth, a stack of papers in his right hand, and this brutally shabby briefcase under his left arm.

"Well," I told Amber, "if it makes you feel better, I wasn't calling to compliment you—"

Mr. Hall managed to remove the pencil without dropping his briefcase but not without an awesome effort. "Don't forget, there's a lunchtime editorial meeting today," he said, before the crowd swallowed him up again.

"Not even!" I cried. "Not today."

"You sound furiously distraught," Amber remarked, "and it's not even first period. Were you calling for advice?"

"As if. I just wanted to let De and you know that there'd be a certain Italian Baldwin joining us for lunch. Only I've just been harshly brought back to reality. Mr. Hall reminded me that there's a *Buzz* meeting at twelve-thirty."

"How dope," Amber said. "I'll let the Crew know. I can't wait to share what I'm working on."

I clicked off. I had about two seconds to get to history with Miss Geist. It was too late to catch Aldo now. But I knew from perusing his schedule card that he had phys ed next period. I hurried into history, greeted Miss Geist—who was wearing this long print dress with pouffy sleeves and whose wild auburn tresses were in crucial need of a trim and maybe just the teensiest touch-up—and rushed to my seat to phone Amber again.

"Yes?" she said.

"Amber," I whispered, "ask De if Murray has P.E. second period, okay?"

"Excuse me, who is this?"

"Amber, it's Cher," I said, wondering if a neurologist was needed, "one of your closest friends who just talked to you a minute ago?"

"Oh, I thought it was some random person who was trolling for a messenger service. I mean, I *am* wearing Todd Oldham, Cher." Her voice rose dangerously. "Did you ever see a messenger in Oldham? I don't think so. That should at least be a clue!"

"Amber, be careful. Lower your voice," I started to caution her.

But it was too late. "Whoops!" she shrieked, and the line went dead.

I knew what that meant. Another irate teacher. Another cell phone confiscated. I'd tried to warn her. It was always hazardous to call attention to yourself while conversing cellularly during class. Look at what had happened to De. Obviously there was an administrative crackdown in progress. It was an ugly trend.

But I was desperate. I started punching in Murray's numbers.

"Cher?" Miss Geist was finishing up attendance.

I clicked off and hid the phone. "Present, Miss Geist," I said. "And by the way, I like that little prairie look you've got going. But let's talk hairstyles after class, okay?"

She tossed me a tentative smile, toyed nervously with her locks for a moment, and moved on. "All right, class, let's open our books to page 897: the end of World War Two," she said.

I redialed. "Murray, do you have P.E. next period?" I whispered when he picked up. "There's this new guy who's in your class," I continued after he'd said yes. "I need to get a message to him, and I don't have his number. His name is Aldo."

"He's right here," Murray said. "Hold on."

"Hi, Cher," said Annabell. "Hang on, I'm just passing the phone."

Then Sean said, " 'Sup?" and I whispered to him that there was a *Buzz* staff meeting at twelve-thirty in Mr. Hall's room, just in case he was interested. He thanked me and passed the phone to Aldo.

"For me? I don't understand." I heard his deep bewildered tones. Then a cautious "Ciao?" on the line.

"Ciao, Aldo. It's me, Cher. I am frantically sorry, but something's come up and I can't make it for lunch. Can we catch up later? I'm free between three and three-thirty, I think. How does that look? I can meet you at the bench where I was sitting this morning. Doable?"

"Three o'clock? *Sì*. It's good, yes?"

"Cher?" Miss Geist called. "Are you with us? The significance of August 7, 1945?"

"It's the bomb—" I told Aldo.

"Correct," said Miss Geist. "The atom bomb. All right, now, Summer—"

I clicked off feverishly.

At twelve-thirty we assembled in Mr. Hall's room. I was way gratified to see Sean, Murray, Jared, Summer, Tai, Amber, and De. Baez and Janet had shown up, too. And a few minutes after we got under way, Ringo popped in.

Mr. Hall's eyes got all misty over the turnout. He was so moved, or it could have been his allergies. So anyway, when we were arrayed in this big circle around his desk, and Mr. Hall was perched on the edge of it with his skinny socks all wrinkly around his ankles, which is like a very academic look but so not attractive, he said, "The purpose of this meeting is twofold: to discuss what a journalist is and does; and to choose topics for articles for the next issue of the *Alcott Buzz*."

Sean started to buzz, but we all kind of rolled our eyes or shook our heads, so he shrugged and stopped.

"Let's talk about journalism for a moment," Mr. Hall said, in this way that you knew that a "moment" was so not the time scheme he had in mind. "There are reporters who simply cover events—who recount the circumstances of, say, a fire, flood, earthquake, or even a local charity affair—"

"I object!" Amber sprang to her feet. "How can you equate an upbeat occasion, where people concerned with a poignant issue spend a fortune on viciously glittering attire to party down and get these adorable little gift bags, with a heinous natural disaster?"

"She's right," Annabell said. "A charity function is a totally prime fashion op, which a flood is so not. Have you even seen pictures of flood people? Usually they're like all saving the TV or the dog. You never see anyone wading out of the wreckage clutching a decent Lauren or Donna Karan—"

"My stepmother ran back to save her Blackglama mink when their Vail condo was burning," Baez differed.

"All right. All right, people!" Mr. Hall called. "The important distinction here is not the type of event but the type of reporting. As I was saying, there are those who record the who, what, when, and where of a newsworthy situation. They are reporters. They *cover* events. Then there are investigative journalists, who *uncover* events. Investigative journalists ask why." He paused.

"Why what?" Sean asked.

"Why a particular event happened and what it means. They go deeper than just describing incidents or delivering surface facts. They dig behind the scenes. They look for reasons. They investigate. Can anyone give us an example of investigative journalism?"

"Well, like Woodward and Bernstein," Ringo said.

"Isn't that a steak house?" Baez asked.

"Woodward and Bernstein"—Mr. Hall beamed at Ringo—"were *Washington Post* reporters who investigated a break-in at the Watergate complex and uncovered a plot that actually toppled the president of the United States. So, yes, Woodward and Bernstein are excellent examples. They weren't content with merely reporting a criminal trespass occurrence. They wanted more. They wanted to know why." Mr. Hall looked us over. "What would you like to know more about?" he asked.

Tai's hand went up. "Well, like the grading system in this school, for instance—"

"Yes?" Mr. Hall looked pleased. "Did you have a specific issue in mind?"

"Well, yeah. Like why Ryder got a D on his social studies paper when he copied from Alana and she got a B-plus."

Mr. Hall closed his watery pink eyes for a moment. When he opened them again, he said, "That's an intriguing mystery, Tai, but is it newsworthy? In what way will the answer to that question affect our lives?"

Tai cocked her head thoughtfully, but Mr. Hall did this instant stop sign with his hand. "Please don't answer that now," he urged her. "Just think about it. All of you. And while you're at it, remember that the cardinal rule of journalism is not to be emotionally involved in your subject. A good reporter stands apart from his or her own emotions and observes. Observes and remembers. Observes and records. A good reporter is objective, unbiased, open-minded, and determined to discover and disseminate the truth about a subject or issue. As

Woodward and Bernstein helped reshape our nation's political history, so every honest journalist can help to change our world."

Mr. Hall's little talk was way inspiring. I burst from my seat and began to applaud him. To change, to reshape—these were not just words to me; they were my way of life. I resolved to become the best reporter I could be, one who lived up to the highest standards of journalism.

"Thank you, Cher." Mr. Hall blushed adorably and motioned for me to sit down. "Now, I'm not saying that reporters are totally objective," he continued. "The best reporters also have what we call a nose for news. Does anyone know what that is?"

"Ask Amber," Murray suggested. "She's got a nose for every occasion."

"Do not even dignify that remark," Dionne cautioned Amber. Then she turned her blazing hazel orbs on Murray. "Typically childish male one-upsmanship," she said. "Whenever boys feel uncomfortable about a topic or don't understand what's being said, they resort to insults and other brutally lame retorts."

The boys all went, "Oooooh."

"You got played," Sean called to Murray.

Mr. Hall got everyone to settle down. Then he went on for a while about how to write our articles, like how to organize them, how to conduct interviews, and how a story had to have a hook or a handle, some issue or topic around which to focus. Finally he said, "Now let's move on to your assignments. First drafts are due on Monday."

"Monday? That's less than a week away." Amber's nasal whine led the groaning and grumbling choir.

"A week is more than ample. Many of our finest columnists have daily deadlines," Mr. Hall reminded them. "Now let's talk about the pieces we'd like to tackle."

I raised my hand.

"Yes, Cher?" Mr. Hall called on me.

"As chief correspondent, I have some thoughts on this matter," I announced. "Here's the way I see it, Mr. Hall," I said on my way to the blackboard. "If I may . . ."

I drew four blank pages on the board. "Let's look at both form and content," I proposed. "I think Sean can handle the sounds column for this issue, a page-three feature." I tapped the appropriate page, drew a column length on it, and scrawled in Sean's name. "Amber's got the science beat covered with an enlightening update on cosmetic surgery." I circled a section on page two.

"I'm supposed to describe the latest surgical enhancement procedures in that meager space? Not even!" Amber protested. "Explaining the nose issue alone could fill a column."

"Don't get snotty," Murray quipped.

I ignored him. "Hel*lo*. This is not inscribed in stone, Amber. See?" I demonstrated. "This is chalk in my hand—"

"Technically, it is stone," Ringo interrupted, cleaning his wire-rims with a pocket hankie. "Chalk is a soft white powdery limestone consisting chiefly of fossil shells or foraminifers—"

"Fossils? Eeeuw!" Summer squealed. "Like little dead dinosaurs and stuff?"

"Which brings me to my next suggestion," I said. "Which is that Ringo and Janet work up a fun quiz for the math geeks and cyberdweebs crowd. De and Murray have graciously agreed to champion opposing views on a way controversial psychosocial topic. Front-page stuff. Summer, I know you feel strongly about animal rights, so why don't you tackle that issue? And, Tai—"

She waved her hand desperately. "I can't write, Cher. Honest, I get brutally tongue-tied on paper."

"But your graphic skills are solidly awesome," I pointed out. "Didn't you do the Marvin the Martian representation that inspired Ryder's ankle tattoo?"

"I've always admired your notebooks, Tai," De said, jumping in supportively. "Excellent doodles. Museum-quality."

"So I thought you could like art-direct this issue," I continued. "You know, toy with the layout; solicit illustrations, cartoons—"

"You guys!" Tai grinned gratefully. Her bitten Vamp black nails flew to her chest. She patted her heart. "You're the best."

I made a note to myself to discuss the virtues of nail extensions with her. I thought she could start with French tips and move forward to full juliettes. Also, the Chanel Vamp thing was so last year. Then I put down the chalk and said, "Well, that's it. Those are my thoughts."

Mr. Hall's jaw was all unwired. He snapped it up into a

smile. "Well, thank you, Cher," he said as I returned to my seat. "That was a very carefully thought-out presentation."

There was scattered applause. Murray, Sean, and Ringo reached out and gave me low fives as I passed them. De hugged me. "Way stirring," she said.

"Does anyone have anything to add?" Mr. Hall was asking. "Any further discussion or comments?"

"I do." Amber unwound her pea green Oldham-flocked limbs and stood up. "Is there a minor yet glaring omission in these suggestions? I think so. Like what article is Cher going to write?"

"That's a fair question," Mr. Hall said, when everyone started to hoot and throw paper and stuff at Amber. "A good observation. Thank you, Amber."

"I'm totally open to suggestions," I said.

"People? Amber? Any suggestions?" Mr. Hall asked.

"Well, personally," Amber said, "I enjoy features on interesting people. *Vanity Fair* has done some important pieces on denim hunks like Brad Pitt and Matthew McConaughey, and *Sassy* once had this memorable spread about lead singers who spark fantasies, which I found seriously informative. Like it told that Gavin Rossdale of Bush has this Hungarian sheepdog that's like his best bud."

De started frantically waving her hand. "Oooh, I know, I know," she called out. "How about a 'Baldwins in the News' piece? There's this chronic new guy at school who Cher could write up—"

"Aldo. I like it," Amber offered. "You could build a

nimble fashion item around the boy. He's a wicked dresser, Mr. Hall, brutally next-generation."

"A feature on Aldo Belloguardia?" I mused, intrigued.

But Mr. Hall was shaking his head. "I don't know," he began. "A personality profile is interesting, but I think our readers deserve something more substantive, something that goes beyond, er, hunkdom and haberdashery. We'd need a better angle, a more serious focus for the story."

"Well, he's Italian," said De, "so it would be more than just like a big empty oh-he's-such-a-hottie thing. It could be, you know, so educational."

"That's a start," Mr. Hall agreed.

"I could spend hours interviewing him," I said, warming to the plan.

"I'm not just talking interview." De was way excited. "I'm talking serious investigative journalism."

"Girlfriend!" I enthused. "How excellent is that idea? I bet I could come up with like a frantically deep angle. Something that would really spark interest and excitement. Like I'd have to do research, get background info on the boy, dig up sources, use paid informers if necessary—"

"Ryder would die to like be a paid informer!" Tai was getting all psyched, too.

"You'd have to get brutally close to him," Janet crooned.

"Intimately involved," Baez said.

"Intimately," I echoed. Suddenly, my enthusiasm wilted like hot-rolled hair in a rainstorm. Mr. Hall had said that a truly excellent reporter could not be emotionally involved in her subject. So how could I date Aldo and interview him, too? Did I really have to choose between love and career?

That seemed so retro. I mean, here we were on the cusp of the millennium. Wasn't the whole point of being a now Betty having it all? And then it came to me: I'd just have to prioritize! First, I could be this fiercely significant investigative journalist. And after I'd uncovered all the *whys* about Aldo and helped to change his life, we could focus on a brutally buff relationship.

"Well, everyone," Mr. Hall said, "I think we've got the makings of a provocative issue here. And, Cher, if you think you can find the right angle for a truly interesting and informative article about our new student, well, I throw down the gauntlet and say go to it."

"Thanks, Mr. Hall," I said. "I think."

Chapter 7

*P*romptly at three, De and I stood at the top of the school steps. Over the heads of our milling classmates, I searched for Aldo. The Quad was awash with the usual end-of-day chaos. Groups clustered making shrill conversation, Frisbees soared overhead, in-line and board skaters hopped onto handrails and dived down the gracefully curving lawns, cars were being brought around front for the licensed among us. . . .

"Wow, whose wheels are those?" De asked, lifting the new Versace wraparounds she'd picked up at Santa Monica Place and gazing in bare-eyed admiration at a silver Rolls Corniche idling in the shade of an immense royal palm.

"Totally decent," I agreed. "Maybe Paroudasm's father came to pick him up."

"Not even," De said. "Parou's family doesn't do Rolls-

Royce anymore. Not since his dad had this blowout with Britain."

"Britain, as in Great? You mean like the entire country?"

Dionne shrugged. "That's what I hear. Now, that," she added, pointing with her perky chin, "is a real chauffeur's uniform."

A man had emerged from the front of the Corniche and was studying the student body. He wore white gloves and a dove gray ensemble that included a visored cap and tailored trousers tucked into immaculately shined midcalf boots. De was brutally correct. Whatever the Gucci guy might have been, this one was a serious chauffeur.

"Murray and I are going over to Dutton's bookstore in Brentwood to research our piece," De moved on. "They've got a surprisingly deep psychology and philosophy collection."

We started down the steps and were nearly knocked over by Ryder, who came to an abrupt screeching halt on his skates and grabbed on to De for balance.

"Get off me," she shrieked.

"Hey, Cher. Hey, De." Our friend Annabell, daughter of the polo patron, paused on her way up the stairs. "Summer told me what a righteous meeting you guys had. I'm helping her with her *Buzz* article. We're going to pick up some literature at the Body Shop."

"The Body Shop?" De said.

"They're rabidly against animal testing," I reminded her.

"That is so lame," Ryder commented. "How can you tell which animals are smart if you don't test them?"

"Bail, Ryder," I ordered. He released De and went clacking down the stairs.

"There's Murray," Dionne said. "And look who's with him."

At the bottom of the steps, near the bench where I said I'd meet him, Aldo was slapping Murray a high five. The afternoon sun gleamed on his golden face and streaky slicked-back hair. His crisp blue shirt was open at the collar, and his cashmere sweater was knotted casually over his broad shoulders. Yet even in dishabille, he was monster props. A viciously golden hottie.

"Let's go, Miss Dionne," Murray hollered to De. "No time for chillin' with your homies now. We got a date to debate."

"We also got the date, yes?" Aldo called, grinning.

I hesitated. "Well, it's not exactly a date," I explained. "It's more like an appointment."

Aldo shrugged and laughed. Then we all started laughing. It was this totally photogenic moment like you see in depilatory ads. A couple of jammin' babes being teased by their guys in some generic fun setting under a chronic blue sky.

"That boy is furiously fine." De gave me a peck on the cheek. "Beep you later, girlfriend. We are Audi."

"I'm sorry I wasn't able to meet you at lunchtime," I said as Aldo and I strolled toward the bench. "Mr. Hall called this meeting of the newspaper staff. And anyway, I want to talk to you about this story I'm going to—"

"I am also sorry," Aldo cut in. "And I would like still to have lunch. Or maybe even better we go to dinner, yes?" He raked back a fallen blond lock and pinned me with dark smiling eyes. "Is good on Friday? After the school? Maybe we go to a movie?"

Yes! I was thinking, as I checked my organizer to see if the day was clear. Between now and then I'd have plenty of time to prep for the interview, get better acquainted with things *italiano*. And how decent would a dinner with Aldo be? Not just for our maturing relationship, but it would be like a perfect time for me to pump him for the profile. And then I'd have all weekend to write my *Buzz* article.

I closed my electronic appointment book. I had nothing urgent on for Friday. A dental checkup, which could be changed in a speed-dialed second. Oh, and Amber and I had a tentative to tour a stretch of Beverly Boulevard where a flock of rave designers had recently opened shop.

Fragments of a dozen articles on how truly low it is to blow off your female friends when a boy with a better offer comes along danced in my head. None of them seemed actually relevant. I mean, I wasn't dumping Amber for some random romantic interlude; my appointment with Aldo was journalistic. Amber would understand.

Or not. If worse came to worst, I'd lend her my silver lambskin boot legs by Michael Kors.

"All clear," I said. "Friday for dinner is trippin'. And excellently convenient since I want to interview you for a piece I'm thinking of doing for the school paper." Having tucked away my organizer, I looked up.

Aldo's grin was gone. He wasn't even looking at me. Following his troubled gaze, I saw that he was staring at the uniformed chauffeur, who seemed to be signaling to him.

"Someone you know?" I asked.

He turned to me with a start. His warm face had gone cold. He seemed at a loss for words.

Immediately, the back door of the Rolls opened. A slender leg in a white silk stocking and a towering Jourdan pump showed itself. A gloved hand beckoned. A husky female voice called, "Aldo, *caro*, come. *Vieni*."

Aldo bit his lip. Looking frantically unhappy, he said apologetically, "I am . . . *domani*. Tomorrow. I see you tomorrow, *cara*. I must go."

"No problem," I started to say. But he gripped my shoulders suddenly and kissed me gently on both cheeks. Then, waving ciao, he jogged off toward the Rolls.

I waved good-bye with one hand; the other went instinctively to my cheek, as though I could hold on to the warmth of his kiss. But my transition from basic Betty to chronic journalist had already begun. As the sleek silver vehicle cruised off, I noted its L.A. license tag: SB FAB. Talk about a vanity plate.

I was way perplexed, yet furiously intrigued and excited, too. A question had formed in my mind. And I knew that the answer to it would provide me with the heart of my *Buzz* article on Aldo. At dinner on Friday I could fill in the who, what, when, and, where of my profile, but now, like every quality investigative reporter, I had a why to uncover.

I watched the big Corniche disappear down the palm-tree–lined boulevard. And why, I asked myself, had a limousine picked up a certain hottie one day and a monster Rolls-Royce scooped him up the next?

I hurried home fully pumped at the prospect of investigating the vehicular mysteries of Aldo's life. But by the time I slipped my key into the bronze latch of our mammoth front door, my head was all into list-making for my Friday fete with the enigmatic Baldwin. There was so much to do. That is, if I wanted the interview segment of our tryst to be truly successful. Which I seriously did.

"Hello, everyone, I'm home!" I called, before heading upstairs. There was no answer. Which I so hate. I mean, okay, Daddy is an extreme workaholic. But that's why, in addition to landscape gardeners, pool persons, and others on staff, we have Lucy full-time. It is majorly pathetic if you live in Beverly Hills to come home to an empty house. There is no excuse for latchkey kids above Sunset.

"Lucy! Luce, where are you?" I tried again.

"Up here," she called from the second-floor landing. "What are you doing home so early?"

She was peering over the wrought-iron banister at me. "What are *you* doing in my baby-blue shearling vest and Anna Sui knit scarf?" I asked.

"Your room is cold." She sounded annoyed.

"Yes, and the reason you were in my room is . . . ?"

"The TV in the den is broken," Lucy explained impatiently. "And it's too bright in the kitchen to see the screen, even if the set in there wasn't so small."

"So you were watching television in my room?"

"It wasn't worth it," she reported, removing my scarf and vest on her way downstairs. "That guy on *All My Children* with the gray beard and black eyebrows was supposed to get shot today. But of course the gun jammed. I should have known they'd never kill him. His picture was on the front of *Soap Opera News* last week."

She handed me my clothing. "Your father called and left a message on your machine—he won't be home for dinner," she said as I hurried up the stairs. "Since it's just us, I was going to order in."

"That works for me. Try Matsuhisa for Japanese," I suggested. "No, wait." I had research to do. "Let's go Italian tonight. Find out if Trattoria Amici on Doheny delivers."

Lucy had left a couple of kernels of popcorn for me in a bowl on my bedside table. The calorie count didn't seem worth it. I dumped both plump pieces into my desk-side wastebasket, then clicked on the CD remote and let the acoustic angst of the Goo Goo Dolls wash over me.

My brain was so busy it was like an Advil commercial. I dialed Dionne. And while I waited for her to pick up, I grabbed my Montblanc and a personalized notepad, which has this pale floral backdrop that almost totally

71

matches the Laura Ashley pattern on the dust ruffle and window treatment in my room. I made a note to purchase a CD of Pavarotti or the other chunky tenor singing in Italian. Daddy and I had caught their outstanding L.A. performance. It was a brutally popular event. Like all these faces in the news were milling around outside ready to mug you for a ticket. We were seated right behind Frank Sinatra and his wife. And the whole time Frank was like humming along.

To ensure the success of my dinner with Aldo, I needed two things: a spectacular new ensemble for myself and solid background on the boy, which meant steeping myself in Italian culture. The Pavarotti disc fell into the latter category. I mean, Johnny Rzenik of the Goo Goos is attractive, but his music wasn't going to move me forward in my endeavor.

"Hello?" Dionne was on the line.

"How's your language-and-gender research going?" I asked.

"Superfine. I'm at the bookstore right now, and I am learning so much," De said. "There are tons of books available on this topic. It's like a complaint genre unto itself. It makes me feel so connected, you know, realizing that I am not alone with my problem. Plus the people here are frantically helpful." She lowered her voice. "Especially this one raging hottie with sun-ripened dreads who did his freshman English paper on this very subject—*in college!*"

"What happened to Murray?"

"His evil twin, Sean, joined us. They're grunting and bonding over in the magazine section—you know, browsing vehicular publications and snapping on the male muffins in *GQ*. High school boys are so *young!*"

"Especially those of the American persuasion," I agreed.

"Brutally. So, girlfriend, are you going to do the piece on Aldo?"

"For sure. That's why I called." I sat cross-legged on my extra-firm king-size bed, surrounded by the antique silk pillows that George, my interior designer, had picked up at Odalisque, where Madonna sightings are way frequent. "De, I've got so much to tell you," I said. "First of all, he asked me out."

"I'm dying," she said. "That is so buff."

"We're having dinner—which will provide a viciously convenient venue for my interview. I told Aldo I was writing him up for the *Alcott Buzz*—although he appeared to be way distracted when we spoke. He's bitterly mysterious. De, that Corniche we spotted loitering on the school grounds? Aldo bailed in it."

"Not even," she gasped. "Just like the black limo?"

"Just. And as both a reporter and a woman, I want to know why," I confessed. "But first I've got to do my part. For that, and also to help me select a brutally memorable outfit for the occasion, I'd love your assistance, girlfriend. I thought we could do some research on things Italian."

"Here or at the library?"

"Hel*lo.* I mean like on Rodeo Drive, home of Gucci,

Ferragamo, Versace, Prada, Bottega Veneta. . . . We could combine business with pleasure."

"Excellent!" De was on board. Except that her après-school schedule was congested until Thursday. I thought that was a bit late to begin my background search on Aldo, but I wanted De's support. So I was willing to wait.

On Wednesday I asked Amber if she'd join us. But when she realized that my appointment with Aldo was preempting our totally tentative shopping expedition, she frantically wigged.

We were at our regular table in the Quad, finishing up lunch. And Amber started bitterly quoting *Cosmo* and *YM* articles at me. Then she moved on to a rant about how betrayal and desertion are the hallmarks of a shallow relationship and can even provoke traumas such as hair loss and acne.

It was a nightmare. "This is so not about abandonment," I said, trying to counter her rage. "I have a job to do, Amber."

She tossed her Maxfield-label bottled water into her backpack.

"Girlfriend, we went with you to the body tailors," De said, trying to talk sense to her. "Now it's time for you to support Cher in this extremely worthy cause."

"I just happen to be totally booked tomorrow," Amber asserted. "My organizer is so full that I had to change batteries twice this week. But of course now I can lighten it—by removing 'Beverly Boulevard with Cher' from Friday's schedule." Shouldering her backpack, she signaled for a busboy to remove her tray. "And I don't suppose you need someone as replaceable as me," she asserted, "to tell you who a certain silver Rolls Corniche—bearing the license plate SB FAB—belongs to."

She dropped a meager tip onto her tray and left us.

Chapter 8

*D*e did her best to pry the information out of Amber. To no avail. If you looked up the word *stubborn* in the dictionary, you'd probably see a certain Clairol redhead's smirking face right next to it. So Thursday afternoon we set off on our research bender without her. But with Leon Barnes, the bookstore hunk who'd promised De a copy of his language-and-gender essay and offered us a lift to Rodeo.

At Dionne's insistence, we met him about five blocks from Bronson Alcott—far enough away so that Leon wouldn't see us emerging from a known high school and Murray wouldn't spot us scrambling into Leon's bright yellow vintage VW bug. When I expressed dismay at this plan, De assured me that pragmatism, not romance, had dictated the procedure. She wanted

Leon's college paper, and she did not want Murray going postal over it.

"I totally get that. But, De, no one does five blocks on foot in Beverly Hills," I protested. "We'll probably be arrested. I'll do it because you are my true-blue best bud, but it's a brutal schlepp."

"Like we haven't walked much farther than that at the mall?" she challenged.

"With escalators and frequent purchase pauses," I reminded her.

So anyway, Leon turned out to be way attractive for a brain, especially for a boy-brain sensitive to the ways in which language influences relationships. As De had told me, he had dreads bleached almost blond by the sun, and he also sported this excellent sprinkling of freckles across his mocha cheeks. His cuts were attractively displayed in a tight-chested T-shirt which, although generic, was of a stylish sage shade.

"Rodeo Drive, right?" Leon said as he pulled away from the curb. I'd hopped into the backseat, but I couldn't help noticing that his car was a stick shift. I was frantically impressed. There were like three pedals on the floor and all these gears to deal with. He had to be a college boy, I told myself. Yet something about Leon screamed "surfer" to me—something beyond his Reef sandals and flowing midcalf shorts. "You girls must be black-belt shoppers," he remarked.

"Olympically qualified," De acknowledged. "But today we're on a research mission." Despite her denial, I could tell that Dionne was semismitten. She wasn't in like serious flirtation mode, but her lashes were in full flutter. "Which reminds me, Leon," she said. "Did you bring your communications paper?"

"Oh, yeah. In my backpack." He handed her a well-worn canvas bag.

"So, have you worked at the bookstore for long?" I made small talk while De pillaged the backpack.

"What, Dutton's? I don't work there. I was just hangin', looking for, er, you know, books and stuff. And they've got this trippin' little garden there."

"That's where Leon and I hooked up," De said. Then she found the essay, and her lashes kicked into over-drive. "Leon, you got an A-plus on this! That is so noble. And totally fresh to observe. I mean, that a man would focus on such a sensitive subject is surprising enough. But to do so adroitly enough to pull an A-plus is extremely excellent!"

"Brutal kudos," I commented.

"Say what?" said Leon, looking perplexed in the rearview mirror.

"Kudos. That's like an expression of, you know, praise," I explained. "It's a frantic compliment."

"Oh, yeah. I knew that," he said, grinning gratefully.

Leon dropped us off at the Wilshire end of Rodeo Drive with a remark to De that you would so not expect from an A-plus student of gender issues: "Hey, I gave you that paper and all. Don't I even get a kiss?"

De's lashes came to an abrupt standstill. "Does like 'Not even' sound familiar?" she huffed.

With an angry grinding of gears and a squeal of rubber on asphalt, the bug sped off.

Rodeo Drive is supposed to be this place where you spend money you don't have to buy things you don't need to impress people you don't like, right? Well, that may be the case for some. But to De and me it is an adventure-filled upscale theme park. Like a designer Knott's Berry Farm. A total Magic Kingdom, but where nobody sings "It's a Small World, After All." And just like Disneyland, it's got its own currency—plastic.

Patriotically, De and I hit a few of our favorite American haunts before touring the Italian sector. At Face It, the cosmetics-plus emporium, we picked up little dangly crystal earrings. And Dionne snagged a sheer plum lipstick while I opted for a kinder, gentler petal-pink gloss. Then we discovered that if we put our purchases on one card and found twenty-two more dollars' worth of facial accessories to buy, we'd be eligible for this decent mesh cosmetics bag absolutely free.

So we scoured the store for further goodies. We came away with a chronic new exfoliating soap, these Aussie capsules to mend and shine hair, and excellent new wax strips to remove unwanted body hair at a fraction of the salon price. But we'd maxed out the lowest of Dionne's AmEx cards, and they almost cut it up right in front of us.

Which I find not just embarrassing but cruel and unusual punishment. Like if you're bad at math for a minute, public humiliation is the answer? I don't think so. Anyway, by the time I purchased my perfect salute-to-Italy outfit—a sheer Euro-cool Versace mini-caftan that moved excellently and the classic Gucci cotton-velvet jacket that Meg Ryan modeled in *Elle*—we arrived at our next venue way low on research funds.

We were in the shoe area, trying to calculate the exact amount left on our combined cards, when who should step out of a plush changing booth, about to make another costly fashion error, but Amber.

"Totally tubular to run into you," De said enthusiastically. "But I thought you were booked."

"I am," Amber remarked coolly. "And I am so not the kind of person who toys with other people's feelings by whimsically rearranging my schedule." She cut her eyes at me, then smoothed down the stretch fabric of the dress she was trying on. "Right now I'm considering a major investment." She spun before us.

"Excuse me, but the adage about how good green looks on redheads is brutally mythic," I said, eyeing the metallic chartreuse costume she was considering.

"If it isn't Cher of the style police," she said, holding out her wrists. "Cuff me for browsing with intent to purchase."

"Seriously, Amber," De said softly, "it *is* kind of reptilian."

"How astute of you. It's supposed to be," she said. "It's a faux-lizard, faux-snakeskin kind of thing."

"Well, it looks like a salamander on endive," I said. "Amber, no matter what you think, we are your t.b. buds, your true-blue friends, and have only your best interests at heart. You are gifted with a taut bod and fundamentally decent legs, so the length and cling factor of that garment is not at issue. It's that color."

"Plus Summer would totally hurl at the mock-snake aspect. She's way sensitive to animal rights," De interjected.

"Why don't you slip out of that ensemble—or molt, if you prefer," I suggested, "and help De and me choose some pumps to go with my interview outfit? Then we can like pause for iced decaf skim-milk mochaccinos."

"And I would do that because . . . ?"

I knew what would work, but something inside me balked.

"Go on, Cher," Dionne prodded me. "Say it. Say the magic words."

I shot her a look, but really she was right. Queen Latifah said it best, or spelled it out, anyway, in a word: U.N.I.T.Y. In unity there is strength. So I acquiesed. "Oh, come on," I said.

De rolled her hazel eyes. "Not those magic words, the other ones."

"Okay. Amber"—I took a breath—"I'm sorry," I said.

"And?" De prompted.

"Excuse me?" I objected.

"And you . . . you know," De whispered, "need . . . help."

"As if!" I snapped.

De did her sadly disappointed look.

"Okay. Amber, please join us," I said. "I'm sorry if I was insensitive. And I neee . . ."

"Yes, you can, yes, you can, yes, you can," Dionne softly chanted.

I crossed my fingers behind my back, gulped air, and said, "Okay, so it would be way clean to have the merest soupçon of assistance—"

Amber ran across the carpeted space that separated us and hugged me. "You need my help. I know you do," she said, squeezing me so hard that the teardrop diamond on my chain bit viciously into my clavicle.

"I knew you could do it." De was aglow with pride.

"And anyway," I said, breaking out of the clinch, "if you buy that dress, Amber, you are going to regret it. You'll look back at pictures of yourself and go, 'Oh, no, what was I thinking?' and be bitterly afflicted with buyer's remorse unto your college graduation and beyond," I prophesied.

Amber squinched up her eyes at me. But De gently took her hands. "She's speaking the truth, Amber. Learn to trust."

We picked out a pair of Sergio Rossi satin sandals. But the salesperson refused to let us pay for them one shoe at a time, which we could have done with De and me pooling our credit cards. Finally Amber pulled a Visa Gold out of her wallet and fully saved the day. After which we took a brew break at this nice outdoor café on Santa Monica.

The sun was still warm, and the umbrella tables were stylishly cheery. Plus it was the kind of place that left the Sweet'n Low right on the table instead of having waiters stash it in their pockets to dole out one little packet at a time. Which I think is such an indicator of class. It just says like this isn't the kind of place that worries about someone snagging a packet of sugar substitute. Which some places actually do.

After we ordered our beverages and took turns showing off the purchases in our shopping bags, I tried to get the outing back on track.

"The original intention of this afternoon's trip," I said, tucking an adorable chemise of Tuscan lace back into my Giorgio bag, "was for me to gather reference materials for my upcoming interview. So I suggest that we take a minute or two to share Aldo info. Does that work for everyone?"

Amber and Dionne nodded, so I took out my floral-print notepad and one of the matching pencils that came with it. "All right, then, who wants to begin?"

De said, "I've seen that black limo pick up Aldo twice this week. And each time he acted just as hesitant and jittery as that first time we saw him. Unfortunately I'm no closer now to identifying the man with the cigar, except to say he continues to be a chronic dresser. And upon closer inspection he looks a little like Aldo around the mouth."

I paused in my note-taking. "Could you elaborate?" I asked.

"He's got a space between his front teeth."

"You were that close to him?"

"No, I was in science lab, and I used the telescope. It's furiously powerful. I mean, the man's skin looked like these erupting craters of the moon with humongous black branches bursting out of them."

"Don't go there," I cautioned.

"It was just regular pores and like facial hair, you know, only magnified. Oh, and also, I think you should know that Aldo seems to be bonding with Sean and Murray," she said as our drinks arrived.

"And that is relevant because . . . ?"

De shrugged. "I just thought you should know."

"Thanks, De. That was excellent," I said sincerely. "Amber?" I turned to her.

"Excuse me. Waiter, waiter," she called after sipping her iced cappuccino. "Is this skim milk or one percent?"

Our waiter shrugged his shoulders, which were thin and rounded and made you feel all maternal, like you'd want to yell, "Stand up! Stop slumping!" Also he had this little potbelly that jutted out over his white apron. You wouldn't have expected such a person to be style-conscious, yet he was sporting an eyebrow earring, which I thought conveyed unexpected flair. "I don't know," he said. "Did you want skim?"

"Duh, I guess that's why I asked for it," said Amber.

"No problem," the waiter said, and took her drink back inside.

"Amber!" Dionne was shocked. "First of all, you did not order skim. And secondly, never, never talk to a waiter that way. Or anyone who handles food."

"Why not?" Amber demanded.

"Because they'll spit in your food," said Dionne. "Oh, and Cher, I just thought of something else. I'm pretty sure he's not an agent or other Hollywood insider—the man who hugged Aldo, not the waiter—because you can tell by the license plate that it's a rental limo, not leased or privately owned. Entertainment-industry execs always have their own limos."

"I hate to even raise this possibility," I said, "but might the man be like a gangster?"

"In Gucci, with Granello loafers? Not even!"

"Well, maybe he used a personal shopper," I ventured. "It's not out of the question. Anyway, speaking of license plates"—I turned to Amber, who'd grown pale—"what did you find out about the silver Corniche?"

"He wouldn't dare," she blurted.

"Who wouldn't dare what?" asked De.

"Spit in my skim milk," Amber hissed.

"The waiter? Probably not," I assured her. "So who owns the Rolls?"

"Well, I've seen the vehicle cruising in my nabe. Otto, my trainer, says it belongs to this major garmenta, someone significant in the rag trade."

"Possibly a renowned clothing designer?" De asked.

"All I know is it's some big wheel in the fashion world, a prominent female, but Otto didn't give me her name. Do you want me to pursue the matter with him?"

My mind was abuzz with possibilities. All I'd seen was a well-garbed leg and a gloved hand, yet I was thinking Cindy, Naomi, Elle . . . ? Could one of the aging supermodels have fallen for the boy? "Thanks. I'd appreciate that," I told Amber, pushing my iced decaf latte in her direction. "Here. I'm totally full."

Amber was fiercely grateful. "How could I have doubted you?" she said.

Chapter 9

*T*he Sergio Rossi satin sandals I'd purchased were platforms with about a five-inch heel. So I was going up and down the stairs, trying them out, when Daddy came home. It was early Friday evening. Aldo was due any minute.

"Hi, Daddy," I said. "Lucy's got a nourishing dietetic dinner in the micro for you. I'm Audi in five."

"Not on your life," he said, dropping his briefcase onto the hall table and loosening the classic silk tie I'd picked out for him.

"But, Daddy, I told you about this dinner engagement days ago. It's for school."

"That is not a school dress, young lady. In fact, it doesn't look like a dress at all. It looks like . . . half a nightgown."

"You are so sartorially acute, Daddy. I mean, it's not a

nightie, but it is sort of based on that flowing, sheer lingerie look. And may I say that your three-piece wool nailhead suit is so lawyerly."

"I don't care what your dress is based on. Cher, you can see right through that thing," he asserted, tearing off his jacket.

"Duh, I guess that's 'cause it's totally sheer," I explained. "Donatella Versace doesn't believe in under-stated clothing. I mean, she's all like why even bother, then? And anyway, I've got this excellent velvet jacket to put on over it, which is fully opaque." I pointed out my new Gucci, which was draped over the banister. "Plus I'm wearing a body stocking." Arms out, I twirled for him on the landing. "See?"

Daddy balled up his jacket and tossed it harshly into our spacious white living room. It landed with a thwack on the free-form marble sculpture behind our wrap-around sofa.

"Two points," I said, trying to turn his scowl into a smile. "Tell me if I'm off-base here, Daddy, but you seem unusually stressed. Hard day defending the af-fluent?"

"Brutal," he admitted. "I should never have taken this case. Divorce." He shook his head. "It beats corporate law for pure viciousness."

"I guess," I sympathized. "But Baez's mom has been through multiple divorces. And she's like frantically fond of her exes—especially Baez's dad. I mean, she never even used an attorney."

"You see?" Daddy fumed. "That's what I mean!"

The front doorbell rang. I grabbed my jacket. "I'll get that," I said, trying to hurry past him.

He stopped me. "Fill me in again. Who is this boy? And what does this date have to do with school?" Then he took the Gucci jacket out of my hand. "You left a tag on the sleeve."

I experienced a shiver of dread. It was like a total premonition. But taking a deep breath, I said, "Daddy, you'll really like him. His name is Aldo, he's new in school, and he's brutally polite and dresses like a total grown-up. I'm just interviewing him for our school paper."

Daddy unpinned the price tag. I saw him glance at it. Suddenly he clutched his heart.

"What's wrong?" I cried, fearing the worst. "It didn't cost that much, Daddy. Honest. It was on sale. Seventy-five percent off!" Which was a minor exaggeration but not a heinous lie or anything. I mean, it could have been true if I'd waited three months and if like a button was loose or something.

Basically, Daddy and I have a strong and open relationship. I'm usually very candid with him. But this was a matter of life and death.

Finally I realized he wasn't having a heart attack. He'd just been reaching for his glasses. I plucked my jacket out of his hand, kissed him on the cheek, and hurried to the front door.

"Before you look at the price," I cautioned him, "I want you to know that as a cub reporter, Daddy, my purchases can be viewed as an educational research investment and an excellent tax write-off. Now, I can't wait for you to meet Aldo," I said, throwing open the door.

Before me stood a random high school boy in a baseball cap, an oversize hooded sweatshirt that looked suspiciously Hilfiger, baggy Nautica shorts, and Velcro-fastened Adidas speed trainers. He whipped off his oversize shades and grinned at me. "'Sup?" he said.

It was Aldo.

I slammed the door.

"Who was that?" Daddy asked.

Now I understood what De had been trying to warn me about. Bonding with one's classmates was one thing; costuming down to their level was viciously another. Aldo had been the victim of a radical makeover by the Crew.

"Nothing, nobody," I told Daddy. "Pizza delivery, wrong house. Well, gotta run. Ciao, Daddy. I won't be late." Blowing him a kiss, I slipped out the door.

Preparation is frantically crucial to success. Like if I hadn't broken in my new pumps on the stairs, I'd never have been able to totter across our cobblestone driveway and dive into the cab Aldo had waiting. Not without triggering a painful ankle mishap.

Preparation also prevented me from commenting on Aldo's new look. Every word of Mr. Hall's briefing on professional journalistic behavior was burned into my brain. So I knew, from his "How to Conduct an Interview" segment, that a reporter does not inject her own opinions and values into the story. Plus she's supposed to make the interviewee comfortable.

So I settled beside Aldo in the cab and went, "Whoops, my blunder. Guess I overgarbed. I don't mind Taco Bell at all."

"No, no." Aldo waved off my words. "You look beautiful, perfect. How to say . . . dope, yes?" He gestured at his own clothes, plucking the Hilfiger sweatshirt. "I am the one who should, er . . ." He seemed to be searching for a phrase.

"Apologize? Change? Slip into something decent?" I tried to help him.

"Explain." He found the word. "Yes, later I explain, okay?" Leaning forward, the garmentally impaired hunk gave our driver the address of one of L.A.'s trendiest A-list eateries.

I was like, Tscha! You can take the boy out of cashmere, but you can't take the cashmere out of the boy. The bistro he had chosen was viciously props. The place was noted for serving up heaps of attitude. Yet despite Aldo's severely casual ensemble, we were treated with frantic respect.

The only flaw was that they'd bungled the Baldwin's seating request.

He seemed a speck overwrought by the mix-up. He hunched up his broad shoulders and pulled his baseball cap way low on his brow. You could hardly see his classic face as we followed the maître d' outdoors.

"Really, this is a monster location," I tried to console him. "It totally busts fresh."

Aldo had wanted a table in a quiet corner of the back dining room. But the patio site we were settled in was prime. Our table was on a flower-adorned deck overlooking Robertson Boulevard. A pretty latticework fence separated us from the street traffic. It was an excellent people-watching venue.

"If you like it, then I am happy," Aldo said, trying for a gallant grin. It was a two-thumbs-up performance by a genuine hottie. But I could sense his continued discomfort with our outdoorsy locale.

Nutrition-wise, the Belloguardia babe and I turned out to be hugely yin and yang. It was like flora versus fauna. I went the salad route—Caesar, hold the Parmesan, egg yolks, anchovies, and croutons—while he opted for a carnivorous cholesterol fest featuring steak au poivre.

"I'm sorry you didn't get to meet Daddy," I said as our waiter left us. "The timing was way off. Basically he was like throwing a stroke. The man is so intense."

Aldo nodded knowingly. "My father is the same."

"Really?" I felt like reaching for my notepad right then. But I exercised professional restraint. In keeping with journalistic tradition, I opted to raise Aldo's comfort level with amusing small talk before plunging into the interview segment of our evening. "And yet Daddy is furiously sensitive," I added.

Aldo threw up his hands. *"Esattamente!* Exactly," he said. "Like a child, no?"

"Tell me about it," I remarked. "But he is a renowned lawyer, conscientiously vicious on his clients' behalf. Which can be severely stressful. Especially with this brutal new case he's working on. Usually Daddy doesn't do divorce."

Aldo laughed aloud. "My father also," he said. Then he reached around the breadsticks and took my hands.

"*Basta,* okay? No more. We forget about our fathers now, yes? Cher, I want to know only about you."

"That is so coincidental," I said. "I was actually thinking the same thing." I pulled my notepad out of my classic quilted Chanel. "So like where are you from?"

"Italy, of course." He seemed surprised.

"Of course," I said, jotting it down. "I knew that. But like where? North, south, east, west?"

"North. In Tuscany. Have you ever been to Italy, Cher?"

I shook my head and wrote down "Tuscany."

"I think you would like it," Aldo continued. "Especially where I come from. Tuscany is hill country. There you have fields of poppies and sunflowers, vineyards and olive groves. And everywhere are hilltop towns with walls and towers built centuries ago. Cathedrals and castles from the medieval time."

"That is so enriching. So did you grow up in like a castle or a condo or what?" I inquired, pencil poised.

"No, no. In a farmhouse." I thought I heard this hint of impatience in his response. But his dark eyes were all shadowed by the brim of his cap, so I couldn't actually tell.

"A farmhouse." I wrote it down. "So then your dad's not a lawyer. He's like what, a farmer?"

"Not exactly," Aldo said, straining to see what I had written. "We have also a home in the city." There it was again, not impatience exactly. More like, what, defensiveness?

Our food arrived. "There is totally nothing wrong with being a farmer," I told him, nodding yes when the

92

waiter held a pewter pepper grinder over my salad. "I mean, like did you see *Babe?* Did you love that film or what?"

"Babe?" Aldo tilted back his hat so that I could see his eyes. They were way perplexed. He waved off the pepper, and the waiter left.

"Some people were grossed by it," I continued, picking a black olive out of my greens. "They thought it was a travesty the way the animals were like chatting." He was staring at the olive. "A fatty little ball of empty calories," I explained, placing it delicately on my bread plate.

"Why are we talking about a pig?" Aldo grabbed a breadstick, bit off the tip, then shook it at me. "Babe. *Il porco?* The pig? What are you saying?"

"I was just trying to make a connection. Between farming—which is a frantically worthwhile endeavor, but not necessarily newsworthy—and, say, motion pictures—which my audience would so prefer learning about. So you do know who Babe is." I jotted that down, then pressed the notepad to my chest. "Aldo, I'll be frank with you. I'm desperately trolling for an angle here."

He burst into this agitated Italian soliliquy. Then he said in English, "Why you want to know this? Why are you writing?"

"Hello. I told you at school, Aldo. It's for our school paper, the *Alcott Buzz.* I'm going to do this profile on you. And frankly, this farming slant will so not rock my readers. Plus it rings false to me. I mean, you don't even dress like a farmer. At least, not until tonight—"

"No, no, no," he interrupted me. A busboy brought our bottle of mineral water just then, and Aldo fell silent. He folded his lean, toned arms across his pecs and sullenly sucked on his breadstick.

Whoa, I thought, De was right. Around the mouth and that classic Baldwin jaw, there was a definite resemblance to the cigar smoker in the Gucci threads.

"I'm trying to come up with something truly catchy," I explained when the busboy had departed. "Like if you're a Tuscan movie star or involved in, say, a fashion liaison with a possessive supermodel, or even if you're in some kind of interesting trouble, it would so lend texture to my story."

"I don't understand." Shaking his head, he began to saw into his steak.

"Well, Mr. Hall thinks we need an issue to hang the article on. So I'm trying to find out what about you is massively riveting."

He set down his knife and fork. "Cher, I don't come to dinner for Mr. Hall. I come for you. You understand? I come because you are the bomb. The way fine babe. And because you are so kind to me. But now I believe something is not good."

He began to tick things off on his fingers. "You like this table, here where everybody can see us. Can see *me*, yes? And you tell me your father is a lawyer. And now you write down everything I say. Why? For your father? For my father, too?"

"No way," I protested.

"For my mother, then?" Something in the street

caught his eye. "Aha!" he cried. *"Eccolo che viene.* Here he comes!" He let loose a frantic Italian tirade, then practically shouted, "I know something goes wrong!" Abruptly turning his back to the boulevard, Aldo pulled his hat down over his face and scrunched way low in his seat.

I peered through the latticework. The big black limo with the silvered windows was slowly cruising by. "Who is that?" I asked Aldo. "Why are you so bent out of shape?"

"Why do you pretend to me?" he demanded cryptically. "You know who it is."

"Not even!" I objected.

"Hah!" He threw down his napkin. It was this totally dramatic moment. Aldo grabbed the tabletop. His glittering dark eyes caught and held mine. "As if!" he growled. Only it came out sounding like "Has heef." And though I had no idea what he was ranting about, I found his passionate presentation furiously compelling.

"I totally respect your emotional honesty," I said after a moment. "But, Aldo, the first draft of my article is due on Monday, and we've barely scratched the surface. I mean, I could go way superficial, like I could ask you what's your favorite book and like if you were an animal what would you be. But I'm going for a deeper, more revealing piece. A why, not just a who-what-when-and-where—"

"It's gone?" he interrupted me. "The car?"

"The black limousine?" I checked the street. "It's gone," I said. "Is it yours?"

95

"No," Aldo said emphatically, then added, "No and yes." He took a drink of mineral water, then filled his glass again.

"Cher, here in America, at the school, even at my home, everything is strange to me, new to me. Everything is . . ." He waved his hand, his slender fingers groping the air, as if he could pull the perfect words out of the sky. "Not so good" was what he settled on. "With you, I want . . . good. Just good, you know?"

"I'm frantically in favor of that," I assured him.

"Then why do you ask me everything and tell me nothing?"

"But I told you all about Daddy," I began.

"I don't want to talk about my life, Cher." Aldo had not even paused to take in my protest. "My life now," he persisted, "is . . . whack."

"Transparently," I agreed. "And as a journalist, I'm sure I can help you. I mean, you see these articles every day about people in grievous circumstances, and they just tell their stories to these complaint reporters and the next thing you know, people are sending them turkeys and scholarships and all."

"Turkeys!" I could see the color rising in his velvety cheeks again. His Tuscan tan had reddened to basic brick. "I don't understand you!" he grumbled. "You talk to me about turkeys and pigs, and then you say what an animal I am."

I put down my pad and pencil. "I did not say that you were an animal," I protested. *"Au contraire!"* I wanted to reach across the table and touch those burning cheeks. I wanted to stroke Aldo's hands and tell him how truly classic I thought he was. But I was furiously torn between my feelings for the boy and my obligations as a journalist.

If only I'd chosen another subject to research and write about, I thought, as the waiter began to clear away our barely touched dinners. A topic that was fascinating, poignant, possibly even life-altering, and yet not all that difficult to research; an important story that I was not emotionally involved in.

"Dessert?" the waiter asked.

I shook my head. Although every escapist cell in my body was crying out for chocolate.

"Only the check," Aldo told the waiter. "We are Ferrari!"

"Audi," I whispered.

Chapter 10

Saturday morning, while my hair was in hot rollers, I spent like fifteen minutes trying to trace how my dinner with Aldo had taken such a brutal dive.

I knew that a heinous misunderstanding had taken place. For starters, the Tuscan hottie had been date-oriented, while I was on a career path. There was also the language barrier, though I have to say I was stirred by Aldo's attempt to brighten his dialogue with lively local idioms. Finally, I sensed that the boy was in turmoil and truly needed my help. Yet he couldn't commit to accepting it.

Whatever, I thought. I mean, it is not that the episode wasn't disturbing. I was just so not willing to turn a potentially excellent weekend into a bitter angstfest.

So the rest of the time De, Amber, and I kicked back and enjoyed life at the top. We did brunch, boutique hopping, and movies in Westwood. Took a spring spa morning at Elizabeth Arden. Checked out the Oldham showroom on Beverly Boulevard; it is the total jewel in his crown. Tested our bikinis and sunblock while screaming in the surf at El Matador. And maintained avid cellular contact with a vast network of like-minded buds.

On Sunday evening I cranked out a rough first draft of my Aldo profile. Although I had poignantly few personal stats and zero revelations about the boy, I did manage some nice images of the Italian landscape, thanks to a library video on the hill towns of Tuscany that Tai had snagged for me. As a first foray into serious journalism, my article didn't brutally blow or anything. I thought it was a good effort. But basically it was light.

I am so not about brooding. By Monday morning I was all, Get over it, Cher. Grab a wake-up cappuccino and croissant at the latte bar, stride across the school grounds greeting friends and fans, and like be open to the opportunities of the new day.

I hadn't spoken to De since the night before. So we were sitting on the bleachers near the tennis courts, catching up, when the first period bell rang.

"Last night, after *Singled Out,* I like clicked off the tube and started reading Leon's college paper," De reported as we strolled back across the Quad together. "Cher, the boy is practically a raging feminist. I never knew a man could be so sensitive. Especially one with monster abs."

"And yet," I reminded her, "his behavior seems brutally at odds with that notion. I mean, he expected like a physical reward just because he gave you an A-plus paper to plagiarize."

"Not even! First, the kiss request had nothing to do with his essay. It was for the lift to Rodeo. And secondly, I have no intention of ripping off Leon's paper. Although I have to say it would be a tragic loss not to lift a paragraph or two. The boy is so articulate and fully collegiate."

"What about Murray?" I asked.

"He's a high school boy, Cher. A total child," De said, pulling Leon's essay out of her stuffed-animal backpack. "Remember Murray's faux-macho stance on apologies? Well, listen to this." De ran an acrylic down the page. "Okay. Here. 'Love doesn't mean never having to say you're sorry. Love means being able to say you're sorry and being strong enough to admit you were at fault.'"

"Leon wrote that?" I was astonished. "That is so deep," I conceded. "It's like poetry."

"It's not just about love," De said triumphantly, "it's about respect."

We slapped a limp high five and hurried up the steps and into the school corridor, shouting, *"R-e-s-p-e-c-t."* Then we kissed good-bye outside Mr. Hall's room, and I rushed into class.

"Glad you could join us, Cher," Mr. Hall said. "You're late."

I dropped my backpack onto my desk and said, "Mr. Hall, everyone with a decent chronometer in this entire school—and I happen to have a classic Rolex in stainless steel with matching Oyster bracelet, which is a totally certified Swiss timekeeper with an outstanding performance record—knows that Bronson Alcott's bell system is brutally archaic."

"I have a Patek Philippe," Paroudasm called out, displaying the wafer-thin gold watch on his wrist.

"Big deal," Jesse Fiegenhut shouted. "My TAG Heuer 6000 series is water-resistant to two hundred meters."

Amber's hand shot up. "Oh, and like what, an eighteen-karat yellow-gold Breitling Chronomat is chopped liver?"

Mr. Hall shut his eyes prayerfully and shook his head. "Sit down, Cher. We'll negotiate your tardy some other time. Right now we're discussing the future of the written word. Ryder, you had some thoughts on this?"

"Not really," Ryder said. "I just wanted to say that I lost my watch, probably in the vicinity of the Venice Skate Park. And while it's not gold or anything, it has like important sentimental value to me. My little brother got it for his eighth birthday, and I just snagged it out of his drawer about a week ago. It's a vintage Ninja Turtles timepiece featuring I think it's like Leonardo, or it might've been Michelangelo—"

I noticed that the seat behind me was empty. But before I could dial De to report on Aldo's absence, the Baldwin himself rushed into class wearing these Black Fly shades that hid half of his outstanding face. "*Scusi . . . perdono.*" Whipping off the sunglasses, he hurried up the aisle. "Sorry, to be late, but I . . . er—"

"Spare me, Aldo," Mr. Hall said, cutting into Ryder's testimonial. "Just take your seat."

Aldo was again outfitted in oversize urban street wear. But nothing could disguise his hunkdom, which was now accessorized by way attractive facial stubble. Clearly, boy and razor had not connected over the weekend.

With a sincere and unrestrained smile, I whispered ciao and waggled my fingers at him. Something told me, however, that those golden bristles accenting his jaw were more a matter of emotional distress than a fashion statement.

In a gesture that had become familiar to me, Aldo raked back his sandy blond curls and grinned endearingly. "I must speak to you, yes?" he said, slipping into the seat behind me. "After the class?"

I put away my cell phone and checked my organizer. "Doable," I concluded.

"So most of you believe that the written word—books, newspapers, magazines—is antiquated," Mr. Hall was saying. "Or 'way ancient,' as Jared put it. And that other media—television, CD-ROMs, the Internet—are taking over as our primary means of communication?"

"You can find out more, faster, and it's way more amusing on the tube," Lorenzo agreed.

"Yeah, like with this issue of the school paper we're supposed to be putting together," Baez explained, "wouldn't it be word if instead of compiling yet another sleep-inducing edition, we could do like one of those manic TV newsmagazines?"

"That'd be chill. And what, like broadcast it over our closed-circuit TV channel, right?" said Sean.

"I have this exceptional anchorperson ensemble,"

Amber announced. "Of course, I've already worn it once this year."

"Yo, yo, yo." Murray was enthusiastic. "It'd be like 'Live from Beverly Hills . . . it's the *Bronson Alcott Buzz.*'"

"Slap me one." Lorenzo leaned across Baez and gave Murray a congratulatory high five.

Summer said, "And it would be all live-action segments. Like instead of Murray and Dionne doing a drab point-counterpoint type of thing, they could have this awesomely interactive debate."

"Oh, that would be novel." Amber rolled her eyes. "You mean like they do now in front of the entire student body practically every day?"

"Yeah, but the audience could join in like on Sally Jessy Raphael," Tai suggested.

"Eeeuw!" Summer squealed. "That show is totally pro-freak. Bitterly imbalanced toward low-end psychopaths. Plus those red-rimmed glasses are not just last year, they're last millennium."

"MTV news rocks," Jared mused. "I'm down with that format. Rapid, visually appealing sound bites, hottie anchors, a bias toward consumer youth."

"I myself am a *Hard Copy* fan," Janet confessed. "Demographically, it bridges the gap between Sally Jessy and Jenny McCarthy—you know, the pace is fast. You've got your attention-grabbing jump cuts with just a trace of substantive content. Like grainy telephoto shots of Princess Di sunning interwoven with, say, aircraft tragedies."

"Excuse me. Hel*lo.*" I stood up and called for attention. "I want to say that I think we're all heading in a very exciting and creative direction here. The idea of producing a televised infotainment instead of our traditional newspaper is massively golden. And if you agree, Mr. Hall, I think we can pull together and pool our rich resources and literally make this dream come true."

The cheers and shouts were so loud they almost drowned out Ariel's frantic yip: she'd been curling her eyelashes and like caught a fold of lid skin in the squeezer.

Mr. Hall silenced everyone. "Well, class, your enthusiasm is certainly heartening. I've rarely seen you people so animated, except when you want a grade changed or are trying to talk your way out of a tardy. To answer your question, Cher, I'm certainly not opposed to the idea. I just question whether it's practical."

"Solidly," I said. "As you all know, Alana's father is a renowned network news anchor. And while he lives on the other coast, he and Alana are emotionally very close. He would do absolutely anything for her. Right, Alana?"

"Absolutely anything." Alana stood and acknowledged a sprinkling of applause.

"So, if we're serious about this, I think Alana can persuade her father to underwrite a Bronson Alcott closed-circuit news show."

"No problem," Alana said. "He missed my birthday party because of some random Asian nuclear calamity last month, so he's already choked with guilt. He owes me."

"Really?" Mr. Hall said. He was so cute and amazed. "Your father would finance this idea?"

"And get a huge tax break," Ringo reminded us.

"I'm thinking a *Vogue*-meets-*Vibe* kind of format," I proposed. "Fashionable yet funky. With the kind of talk-TV feel that Murray and Summer suggested, but with Tai's audience-participation edge. So all we have to do now is put together some jammin' segments on subjects of vital concern to the Beverly Hills adolescent community. We'll want to create a show that's enticing, impactful, and fun," I concluded.

"Yes!" Amber was majorly psyched. "Just like the Home Shopping Network."

I dialed De on my way out of Mr. Hall's room. "I have the most awesome news," I told her.

"Not now." She sounded tense. "I don't want to risk another cell phone confiscation."

"My heart goes out to you," I said. "But technically we're between classes now. Are you sure the ban includes corridor conversing?"

"I can't chance it. I need my phone, Cher. You have no idea how deprived, how empty, it feels to be cellularly bereft. Meet you in the cafeteria fourth period."

"Dionne, wait," I said. "I think you may be the victim of a brutal First Amendment violation. We're treading on freedom of speech turf here." But she'd clicked off. "Be brave, girlfriend," I whispered, and, snapping shut my mobile, left the classroom.

Aldo was waiting for me. He was idling with Murray,

Sean, and Jesse in front of the Crew's lockers. His dark eyes frantically sparked at the sight of me. *"Arrivederci. Sono Audi."* He slapped high fives all around and hurried to my side.

"I've got algebra next. Where are you heading?" I asked.

"I don't care. I must . . . This is so hard for me. Cher"—he took my hands in his—"I must talk to someone. I am away bum."

"Way bummed," I suggested.

"Sì, way bummed," he said gratefully. "So you will help me?"

I pondered the consequences. Being late to Hanratty-the-phone-snatcher's class meant inviting big-time trouble. Clearly the woman had gone hormonal. There was no reason to believe that she would treat me any better than she had De or Amber. The math maven was on a rampage. I had to weigh that fact against the desperate but not unattractive neediness of a brutal Tuscan babe.

No contest.

"I'm going to be late to class," I said, "but okay. Let's talk."

"Mille grazie, thank you." Aldo steered me to the side door and held it open. As we walked together down the shaded steps near the sports center, he said, "I feel I am bugging. I must talk, but it is hard for me to . . . to trust, you know?"

"How grueling. Aldo, as a journalist I am prepared to promise you off-the-record confidentiality," I assured him as we sauntered in the direction of the polo field.

He cocked his Baldwin head at me.

"Loosely translated, that means I won't report what you divulge to me. And just as a person—well, not *just* as a person but as a young, attractive, bright, and popular person with severe expertise in the advice-giving arena—Aldo, I am massively interested in your welfare."

"Thank you. We can sit? Let's rest here." He led me to the empty bleachers overlooking the tranquil polo turf, which was perfectly groomed except for the occasional fly-blown remembrance of ponies past.

We sat together, I in the fourth row where a gentle breeze brought with it the earthy scent of the nearby stables and the far-off shouts of a football scrimmage, Aldo a step below, looking up at me with those velvety eyes. Sunlight glinted off his fabulous blond facial bristles and the oversize shades pushed up onto his streaky hair.

"Tell me everything," I urged. "Starting with that outfit."

"It is my disguise," Aldo said sheepishly. "I try to look like everyone. To not be the standout. So they will not find me."

"That is so excellent," I said. "I thought you'd suffered a grievous style lapse. I should have known that only way grave danger could push you that far over the fashion edge. So like who are you hiding from? Is it some merciless Gucci-garbed troublemaker? Or like a scorned woman with a fatal attraction?"

"My parents," Aldo said.

"Excuse me? Your parents?"

"*Sì*, yes. It's true. They are driving me *pazzo!* Postal."
He leaped to his feet and pounded his chest with open
hands. "They make me crazy! They are making the
divorce, and I am"—he gestured to the scrimmage
taking place in the distance—"the football."

"They're fighting over custody?"

"He doesn't want me to stay with her. She doesn't
want me to go with him."

"So wait. Then the black limo is your dad's? No way!"
I was shocked. "The man so does not look like a
farmer."

"He is no farmer. My father is a banker; he works in
Florence. My mother, she designs fabrics. She is very
famous in Italy. You have heard of Simona Biagi Fabrics?"

"Of course. One of her bathing suits was at Neiman's
the day of the purse-snatching. SB FABI Duh," I said,
lightly slapping my brow. "Of course." Now the license
plate made sense. "She has this awesome silver set of
wheels, right? Rolls Corniche? But, Aldo, I thought you
said you lived on a farm."

The boys' P.E. class meandered onto the polo field,
buckling their riding helmets. They paraded past us on
their way to the stables. Most of them had their mallets
tucked stylishly under their arms. But a few, specifically
Ryder and his slacker pal Ozzie Frost, were messing
around with those lethal, long-handled hammers. They
were fencing and hollering, "*En garde*, man," and
"Parry and thrust, dude."

"Not on a farm with pigs and sheep," Aldo was

explaining. I turned back to him, which was as refreshing as a free spa day. "But yes, in a seventeenth-century stone farmhouse in Tuscany. Of course, it has been enlarged and renovated. And we have olive groves and lemon trees and gardens." He sat back down with a thump. "But no more. It is my father's house. And I am here now, with my mother."

"Fore!" Ozzie shouted. He was near the stables, pretending to play golf now. He whacked a wad of earth into the air with his mallet.

"It's a high pop fly." Ryder tossed away his mallet as if it were a baseball bat and ran backward to catch the flying patch of sod.

"My mother, she is American," Aldo continued. "Well, she is born here. But most of her life she lives in Italy. Now she brings me here to make the divorce with my father. We are here in California two weeks, maybe, and on the first day I go to school, my father comes—from Italy he comes!—and says to me he wants to take me home. Of course, I tell this to my mother. *Eccola!* She drives by the school every day now. If she sees me talking to my father, she . . ." He groped for the words, then threw up his hands.

"Goes ballistic?" I offered.

"Esattamente. Exactly!"

Suddenly Ryder went, "Eeeoww!" I glanced toward the stables.

"What is that all over your hands, man?" Ozzie was staring at Ryder in horror. "Oh, man, bummer. That's like not dirt, dude. It's . . . Whoa, like my mistake."

Carefully, Coach Mitchell grabbed Ryder by the shoulder of his Team Bronson Alcott sweatshirt and began to walk him back toward the gym.

"And my father. He is like your father. As you said, intense but like a child. No one in all the generations of his family has ever been divorced."

"Not even!"

"Never. In Italy, for thousands of years there is no divorce. Now, yes. Since I am born, yes. So he is very, very upset. He wants me with him all the time now. He is become—"

"Brutally possessive?"

"*Sì*. And on Friday I was supposed to spend the weekend with him. He asked me to go directly to his hotel after school. But I want to be with you. So Murray and Sean they give me the clothes. They make me disguised. So if maybe my father sees me with you, he will not—"

"Furiously freak out." I finished the thought. "And that's why you wanted a table inside the restaurant?"

Aldo nodded, then took my hand. He studied it silently for a while.

"I'm hitting the nail rehab after school and getting that pinky repaired," I said, trying to lighten the somber mood. It didn't work.

"I don't know what to do," Aldo confessed.

"Well, now I understand why you practically hurled when the black limo cruised by. But what was that whack rant about me taking notes for Daddy?"

"Forgive me. But when you tell me about the divorce

case your father is working on . . ." He shrugged and looked up again. "Cher, my father tells me that my mother has hired the most vicious lawyer in America."

"Whoops." I took back my hand. Then I thought it over. After a minute I said, "Los Angeles is totally teeming with vicious attorneys, Aldo. Although Daddy is right up there at the top of the heap. So this may just be a bitter coincidence. I'll check it out and get back to you on it, okay?"

"*Sì*, yes. Okay." The dejected Baldwin flashed me a grateful, adorably gap-toothed grin. Yet I sensed the paralyzing misery still racking him. The boy was in brutal overwhelm.

"Aldo . . ." This time I took his hands, which were warm and strong, yet as silky as if he used the exact same moisturizing lotion as mine, a specially formulated hand-care cream enriched with these multivitamins and coenzymes that deliver an extra phase of elasticity and moisture.

"You've got to remember you are in Beverly Hills now," I assured him, "where divorce agreements are prenuptial, and thousands of your peers have learned how to milk happiness—not to mention loqued-out wheels, high-end trinkets, frequent-flier bonus miles, gold cards, and cash—out of shifts in family structure. Trust me. You are so not alone."

He leaned toward me. Beneath the light yet bracing trace of Eternity by Calvin Klein, there was this heat coming off him like from warm bread. He removed his hands from mine and placed them on my cheeks.

Which I was so glad I'd primed with a revitalizing dual finish creme powder, so luxuriously light it liberated my skin.

Aldo's face went out of focus as it neared mine. Then, way gently but in this viciously effective manner, he kissed me. First on one color-enhanced cheek, then on the other. And finally with brutal tenderness on my astonished lips.

Was this the emotional involvement Mr. Hall had cautioned against? Not even! I mean, how grateful must our nation have felt about Woodward and Bernstein? Okay, so probably the Democrats didn't actually kiss them. But surely, accepting the admiration and affection of those you helped didn't totally compromise your journalistic integrity.

I tried to tell myself that I was a reporter first. And yet when Aldo kissed me, the earth actually shook. There was a pounding, galloping pulse in my ears. "Duck! Duck! Watch out, dudes!" I heard.

Opening my eyes, I saw the sophomore polo team riding by and Ozzie Frost's mallet sailing above the bleachers into the cloudless azure sky.

Chapter 11

I needed a new topic.

I was bitterly committed to helping Aldo. His parents were tearing him apart. They both loved him; they both wanted him. I could utterly relate. Who knew better than I the pain and stress of being sought after?

But as a reporter I was dangerously close to breaking the cardinal rule of journalism.

Then, on Thursday, when the *Alcott Buzz* staff met with Mr. Hall to pursue TV possibilities, I stumbled upon a frantically chronic solution.

"Alana's father has come through for us," Mr. Hall announced. Then he waited while everyone shrieked and stomped and Alana, in this noble one-shoulder white top and Joop! skirt with inlaid diamantés, did this little bow.

When things quieted down, Alana said, "He actually loved the idea. Especially after Ringo got on the phone with him and detailed the tax-shelter possibilities."

"His accountant called me from New York last night," the modest math dweeb acknowledged. "He was fully pro the venture. Nice guy. Competent but not, you know, really creative. I mean he hadn't even considered syndication and merchandising, which could net Bronson Alcott quite a bundle."

"Thank you, Ringo, Alana," Mr. Hall cut in. "And I understand that you, Sean, are working out production details with the staff at our local cable television station."

"It's not all that local." Sean stood. "Actually, the studio is in the Valley. I mean, Murray, Jared, and I had to drive all the way to Burbank—"

It was so bogus. Like Sean didn't know when he said it that everyone would start shrieking and going, "Oh, no, not the Valley. That's way too far. Omigod, did you have to go on the freeway? Oh, no, I can't even think about it."

Give me a break.

Then the three of them—Murray, Jared, and Sean—started waving and making victory signs and going, "It was nothing. Really."

De and I exchanged these looks, like bor-ring. Finally Mr. Hall said, "Thank you, Sean. And you, too, Murray and Jared, for your sacrifice on our behalf. I'm sure it was an alarming ride. Which brings us to the editorial, or program-planning, portion of our meeting. Now, I

114

read through the rough drafts of your articles. And they are quite . . ."

Mr. Hall seemed momentarily at a loss for words. "Rough," he said finally. "Now, I don't want to discourage any of you. Summer, your 'Save the Frogs' piece was . . . very impassioned. But I don't think referring to Mr. Latimer, the head of our science department, as 'the Butcher of Brentwood' truly serves your cause. And, Cher, although your description of the poppy fields between Siena and Orvieto was certainly colorful, we didn't really learn very much about Mr. Belloguardia, the subject of your profile."

"That was a way preliminary draft, Mr. Hall. I've only recently like seriously embraced my topic," I explained defensively, when the major moans and murmurs that had greeted Aldo's name subsided. "I totally get what you're saying, though. You want less background and more Baldwin, right?" I asked. "And a viciously pertinent issue around which to focus the piece."

"Bingo," Mr. Hall replied. "And what I'd like to do today is hear some new story ideas for our televised newsmagazine. Or ways in which the articles you're already working on can be adapted to a video format."

Suddenly I got this spark of a smokin' idea.

De and I both raised our hands. "All right, which one of you wants to go first?" Mr. Hall asked.

"I do." Amber's digits made a fashionably late appearance. "I just want to say that the science-and-beauty piece I'm working on is excellently appropriate for the tube because it involves the way fascinating art of computer imaging, which is so visual. But I've been thinking—"

"I thought I smelled something burning," Sean quipped.

Amber shot him an evil squinchie, then continued. "Originally, I was going to focus on me. You know, show how I'd look with different noses and mouths and stuff. But since I'm already attractive and have previously experienced minor nasal enhancement, I thought, Hey, wouldn't it be fun to enroll someone who really needs aid in this area?"

"And?" Mr. Hall was waiting.

"Like you," Amber said.

There was this coughing fit in the room. The whole class went epidemic. Mr. Hall just stood there, blinking at Amber. Finally he cleared his throat. "That's a very generous thought, Amber, and an interesting project. But I think it would work better with a student volunteer."

"Okay, if you insist." Amber shook her head like poor Mr. Hall didn't know what he was missing. "But I already checked and they can do hair implants, chin enlargements, eye-bag removals, lid lifts, liposuction, and of course contact lenses are always an option."

"I'll think about it," Mr. Hall said. "All right, next . . . Dionne."

De got up. "I think I've found a choice way to dramatize my segment, which, as you all know, is on the effect of language on male-female relationships," she said. "I'm going to have a guest expert on the show. A man who is not only well versed in the field but is also like desperately photogenic. And has these serious biceps you wouldn't ordinarily associate with a fecund mind. His name is Leon Barnes. And he's in college!"

"Leon Barnes." I heard Murray musing aloud. "I know a Leon Barnes. His sister Lena goes to USC with my cousin. . . . Naw." Murray shook his head. "Can't be the man. The only field that boy is expert in is the something-for-nothing sweepstakes."

Mr. Hall was down with De's plan. "That is just the sort of thing I meant, Dionne," he said. "Murray, you might think about bringing on an authority of your own, someone to reinforce your views. Very creative, Dionne, thank you. Cher?"

I stood, smoothed down my fashionably short panne velvet body sheath, and waited for the approving whistles of my peers to cease. "As I said," I announced, "I've been doing intense research for my profile of Aldo Belloguardia—"

The room went rampant again with oohs, aahs, and other affirmations of the Baldwin's hottie appeal. One hopeless Barney even went, "Oh, is *that* what you were doing in the bleachers?"

It was this tragically random remark, way too lame to dignify. Besides which, I was way too psyched about my new idea to get sidetracked into a shame spiral.

"I've found a way to go beyond a conventional personality piece, Mr. Hall," I continued. "I have a topic that I think is seriously relevant. One that nine out of ten students in this school have had to face—"

"Oh, no, not another special on kids flunking driver ed," Amber called out.

"Ignore her," De whispered, "like fashion sense has."

"I'm not talking about the heartache of driver ed," I protested, "or the stigma of being wrongfully refused a personal gold card, or even having your weekly allowance cut to, say, three figures—"

"How can a high school–age person manage on three figures? What is that, like three, four hundred a week? Please." Baez rolled her eyes. "My baby sister on my father's side gets two bills a week for cookies and milk. They live in San Diego, and my dad gave her mother—my stepmother, Elizabeth—this red Porsche she wanted, with this cutting-edge fleece-lined baby seat in it. That woman is so beyond extravagant. I mean, talk about your San Diego Chargers—"

"My first stepfather gave my mother a red Porsche, too," Jesse marveled. "Only my second stepfather racked it up. But it worked out. The insurance money bought Mom some way decent new wheels and two weeks in Acapulco, where she divorced him."

"My ex-stepbrother lives in Acapulco," Ariel added. "He totally hates it. I mean, 'cause he's a redhead like his father and gets brutally blotchy in the sun. But his mom won him in a fierce custody caper. So he has to live there."

"That is exactly what I'm talking about," I said. "It's a subject that has touched the life of practically everyone in this school."

"What, sunscreen?" De asked.

"No. Divorce," I explained. "Custody arrangements. The way kids are treated as property to be divided and awarded to their warring parents."

"Not even!" Janet sneered. "My father begged me to live in New York with him. I go, 'As if! Like first show me the turquoise pool, bubbling hot tub, in-house stables, and red clay tennis courts in your Fifth Avenue condo. Then we'll talk.'"

"Word up," Murray agreed. "When my aunt and uncle split, they got into this rude tug-of-war over my cousin T.J. So he got himself hooked up with a killer attorney and negotiated a deal he could live with: spring break in the Caribbean with his moms; winter treks to Aspen with his pops; whole family reunites for the major holidays in a venue of T.J.'s choosing."

"This is so awesome," I said, barely able to contain my enthusiasm. "Murray, Janet—yours are exactly the kind of stories I want. Upbeat, inspiring, instructive! I want this piece to totally empower our peers who may be going through their first divorce experience—"

"Can anyone be that raw?" Baez challenged. "I went through two stepdads before I was eight." Murmurs of agreement rippled through the room.

I chose to press on. "Kids who feel totally torn up and don't see the possibilities for turning a family break-down into a personal triumph," I continued. "I want to expose the pitfalls and share the power ploys of dealing with parents in marital mutation. So like anyone with a choice separation, divorce, or custody scenario to share, please see me after this meeting. Thank you." I sat down.

Not only was Mr. Hall massively supportive of my proposal, but my casting call was totally mobbed. Before our programming session was even over, candidates began slipping me notes volunteering to go public with their stories.

Annabell was one of them. She'd scrawled the bare-boned details of her custody arrangement on a piece of scented notepaper. I read it and thought: A star is born!

By midday I had to turn off my cell phone because it was ringing off the hip.

I only hoped Daddy was not trying to reach me. I had asked him the night before if the divorce he was handling involved a fashion-industry giant. He barely looked up from the bacon cheeseburger I'd used for leverage.

"No, it's this matron from Bel Air who followed the Charles-and-Diana saga," Daddy said. "She wants twenty-three million and for her husband to address her as Your Royal Highness."

"Do they have children, Daddy?"

"All grown and gone," he had said. "Why do you ask?"

"You know I'm always interested in your career." He'd finally set down the burger. Seizing the opportunity, I cut it in two and put half on my Royal Copenhagen porcelain plate. "And in your health," I reminded him, trying to soften his scowl. "Also, I'm doing this story on children of divorce for Bronson Alcott's brand-new cable news show. And I was wondering if you'd be willing to do a cameo on my segment."

"Call Raoul Felder. I'm much too busy now," Daddy growled, plaintively eyeing my porcelain.

"But, Daddy, I so need an informed and outspoken adult advocate."

"Give me back my cheeseburger," he ordered.

I held my dinner plate out of his reach. "I'm way rusty on litigation, property settlements, spousal support, custody precedents . . ." I said.

"How much time will it take?"

"Fifteen minutes, tops," I promised.

"When?"

"A week from Friday. Then you'll do it! That is so excellent, Daddy."

"Burger," he barked.

"It's yours," I said. "I'm just going to take off these two teensy little strips of bacon. You do not need the glycerides, Daddy. Trust me."

With Daddy in the bag and Mr. Hall and my homies solidly behind the project, I needed just one more thing to really spark my show. Well, two things, technically: Aldo's parents.

"No, no, no, no, no," Aldo responded when I dialed him from Book Soup and broached the subject. He was at his mother's palazzo, which turned out to be located a well-tended mile up the road from Amber's stylish casa.

"It is not possible. They do not even speak to each other," the boy insisted. "They would never agree to appear together. Definitely not on a show about divorce."

Cell phone tucked between ear and shoulder, I was paging through an oversize classic on Italian films while

De and Amber checked out the latest Euro fashion rags. "Aldo, you don't understand," I said, studying this still of Sophia Loren when she was like twenty-something and could brutally eclipse the entire cast of *Melrose Place*. "My segment depends on your parents being there." I shut the book. "I mean wouldn't it be whack if like Ricki Lake did a show on animal rights and not one fur violator appeared? Or Oprah repeated her makeover theme, only no tragically obese women in need of decent haircuts and cosmetic revitalizing even showed up?"

I signaled to my buds that I was leaving the store. "Plus it's a closed-circuit show," I reminded Aldo, reaching for my shades as I stepped into the afternoon glare of Sunset Boulevard. "Viewable only in the classrooms of Bronson Alcott. It's not going to be beamed into living rooms or hotel suites or whatever. So your parents won't even get to see the show unless they're on it. And basically, I'm putting the entire segment together to educate them—"

"Momento. Hold on, please, okay?" he interrupted me, then lapsed into this total Italian libretto. And I realized that he was not alone.

"Is that your mom?" I whispered.

"Sì, er, yes," he said.

"Ask her. Ask her now. Tell her I want to interview her about . . . fashion. Her fabrics. Her career," I said. "You know how furiously fascinating I actually find that field. Oh, Aldo, please, please, please, please, *please.*"

I hate pleading. It can make you appear majorly

needy. Which is so unattractive. And in my case, actually untrue. De and Amber emerged from Book Soup. I did like an I'll-be-right-with-you to them and waited for Aldo's response. He was talking to his mother again, but I had no idea about what.

"Cher." The Baldwin was back on the line. "She says okay. She will do it."

"Yesss! One down and one to go. Aldo, will you call your dad and do like the same thing?"

"You want me to say you are furiously fascinated with banking?" he teased.

"Who isn't?" I said. "Buzz me as soon as the results are in." I clicked off.

"Next?" Amber asked. We looked around.

"It's huge. It's hip. It abounds with sounds." De pointed, and we headed across Sunset to Tower Records, where you could not just buy famous recording artists but totally bump into them. It was a known haunt of Madonna, David Bowie, Sinéad O'Connor, and other aging musical legends.

"I think I just rounded out the cast of my show," I told them, as we swung through the doors into the bustling tuneful hive. "Have you connected with Leon yet?"

"Yesterday," De said. "I thought he'd be like all honored and enthusiastic, but he was way elusive. I said it would totally not be a big deal. I mean, we'd just be discussing his paper, going over material that he was certainly familiar with."

"So did he bail?" Amber asked.

"I resorted to begging," De confessed, shaking her head at herself. "I can't even believe I did it. I went, you know, please, please, please, please, *please.*"

"Dionne, that is so demeaning," I said, then burst out laughing. "Me too. I did the same thing."

"Well, I didn't," Amber said, stopping near the escalator. "I would never beg. I'm basically too proud. I mean, I'd lie, probably. Up or down?"

"Let's ascend," said De. We boarded the up escalator. "So, who did you snag for your computer makeover?"

"No one yet," Amber said. "But I'm open to suggestions."

"Hanratty," Dionne proposed.

"Classic," Amber snickered. They slapped limp high fives.

"Wait a minute. That is a viciously fine notion," I said seriously. "Mrs. Hanratty is the perfect imaging redo. I bet it would give her a raging lift at this dire moment in her life cycle. How old do you think she is?"

Amber shrugged. "Anything above thirty-five loses me."

"Let's see," I said. "Her nerves are shot, her reading glasses are on a chain, she uses a do-it-yourself auburn rinse about every six weeks—"

"She's only pierced each of her ears once," De pointed out, "and has no visible tattoos—"

"I guess she's in that Hillary Rodham Clinton gray area—too old for *Elle,* too young to be carded as a senior," Amber decided. "Which does make her a prime enhancement candidate."

"Right." De laughed. "Now all you have to do is get her to agree."

"So let's see, how did that go again?" Amber asked as we stepped off the escalator.

De and I exchanged glances. Then all three of us cracked up and went, "Please, please, please, please, *please!*"

Chapter 12

Mr. Hall wanted to get a school bus to take us to the cable studio in the Valley where Bronson Alcott's first ever TV mag was going to be taped. But no one would set foot in a bright yellow transport that said "If I'm Driving Too Fast, Call: 555-SKOLBUS" on the back. So we piled into stretch limos provided by our safety-conscious parents and headed to Burbank like a multitude of television personalities before us.

We were herded into this petite studio about the size of my walk-in closet. It had a little stage with two lecterns, just like in Mr. Hall's room, and about five swivel chairs disappointingly upholstered in this dental-waiting-room orange. For the audience, there were metal bleachers separated by an aisle. And at the foot of that aisle, right in front of the stage, was a classic camera on wheels.

Aside from the fact that I was wearing a killer apricot sheath with melon kick pleat, which so did not go with tangerine chairs, the entire setup was raging. We were like awestruck for a moment. Then the TV crew came in and held this brief conference with Mr. Hall, and he got up on the stage and said, "All right, everyone. We've only got this space for a limited time. I think we'd better get started." He looked down at his clipboard. "Dionne and Murray, are you ready?"

"Not even!" Amber erupted. "Mr. Hall, Mr. Hall, where are the makeup people? The stylists? And what about the greenroom, where my guest can wait and like nibble on catered canapés?"

Mr. Hall cleared his throat, then turned to one of the professionals who was clipping this little pin-on microphone to Murray's dressy black T-shirt. "No one ordered anything like that," the man said, totally shirking responsibility.

"Amber, you look very nice," Mr. Hall assured her. "And I don't think your guest will mind waiting right here with us. Right, Mrs. Hanratty?" Mr. Hall winked at her.

"Well, Amber did tell me there'd be makeup and hair people here," Hanratty said irritably.

Mr. Hall's hands gripped the lectern. "All right. First up. Dionne and Murray. Are you two ready?"

"Willing and able!" Murray said with a broad smile that bared not only his gleaming braces but an impressive orthodontic debt as well. "My expert will be here in a minute, so I suggest that Ms. Dionne proceed."

I touched up De's blush, a luminous baby pink that so

enlivened her flawless hazel eyes. "Go, girlfriend," I said, knocking cheekbones with her in a prudent air kiss. I did not want to sully an outstanding makeup job.

De crooked an acrylic at Leon, who was wearing a University of Southern California sweatshirt with the sleeves and collar cut off, tight khaki shorts, and beach thongs. His overextended quads and biceps were oiled and gleaming. As he followed Dionne onto the stage, the cameraman hollered, "I'm getting too much glare off this guy. Anyone got a paper towel or some powder?"

Mrs. Hanratty volunteered to blot Leon.

I thought De gave a four-star presentation. She quoted a lot from the transformational best-seller *Men Are from Mars, Women Are from Venus,* which had transformed John Gray from random therapist to affluent author. He deserves every cent he reaps. *Men Are from Mars* not only shows how men totally misunderstand women but also tells how just by changing a few words here and there, women can get what they want from them anyway.

I have personally read this outstanding book, which has chapters like "Women Are Like Waves" and even lists "101 Ways to Score Points with a Woman." Many of these points are perceptive, like "Give her four hugs a day." But others, like number 66, "Help with recycling the trash," are fully baffling.

De also referred very effectively to Deborah Tannen's book on cassette, *You Just Don't Understand,* another big seller in the field of misunderstanding. All in all, De made the case that men can be grievously unaware of women's needs and that their cluelessness is often verbally revealed.

So everyone was all "Yes!" and "You go, girl," and hooting and applauding. Then De said that not every man was that way.

I couldn't help but glance at Aldo right then. He was sitting with his mother, the famous and maturely attractive fabric designer Simona Biagi. I tried to catch his eye, but he was glancing apprehensively at the door to the studio, as though he expected his father to crash through it at any moment.

My nervous Baldwin had forgotten that his dad was picking up my dad on the way to Burbank. And that for a slice of key lime pie, which Daddy never even realized was made with tofu and soy milk, he'd promised to keep Mr. Belloguardia out of our studio until I sent for him.

As De introduced Leon, who was scheduled to read a few paragraphs from his acclaimed report, the studio door did open. In came this serious bronze Betty with these abundant blond hair extensions. Murray motioned her onto the stage.

"My learned colleague, Murray, will try to prove to you that real men are brutally insensitive," Dionne was saying. "But now, as proof that it is so possible for those with Y chromosomes to understand a woman's emotional and linguistic needs, I give you Leon Barnes—"

But Leon had just noticed Murray's expert ascending to the stage. He totally bugged. His sympathetic smile crumpled like Kleenex. His broad chest collapsed as if someone had stuck a pin in his pecs. You could practically hear the hissing sound of breath and confidence leaking from his once proudly pumped bod. The report from which he was about to read hung from his hand like a limp flag on a bitterly breezeless day.

"Leon," De prodded, "what's wrong?" She looked over at Murray, who was briefing his guest and grinning big-time. "Who is that?"

Murray glanced up at her. "This is Lena Barnes," he announced, "Leon's big sister. She goes to USC. She wrote that paper."

I saw De's denial splinter like glass. She whirled to face Leon. "Is that true?" The brawny bowhead shrugged. "How could someone who's been accepted to college, even a local college, be so heinously fraudulent?" Dionne demanded.

"I just turned fifteen," Leon confessed. "I'm big for my age."

"But, but," De sputtered, "you were driving a car!"

Leon shrugged again. "I've got my permit. I'm allowed to drive with a licensed driver. I was with my mom, and then she left. But then you and Cher got in the car. I figured you guys probably had licenses, right?"

"Cut, cut, cut!" Dionne called. "Mr. Hall, my portion of this program has just been dealt a huge, crippling blow—"

"Excuse me, I believe it's my turn." Carrying this jumble of papers and parcels, Murray proceeded to the lectern on his side of the stage. "Mr. Hall, I think what I have to say cuts to the core of this issue."

Leon slunk offstage, but De held her ground. She

gripped the edge of her lectern and waited, her delicate chin held high, her irresistible hazel eyes misty yet unblinking.

"After extensive research, I have to say that Dionne is basically correct in her argument," Murray announced. "There are strong discrepancies in the manner in which males and females communicate. Take the simple issue of apologizing. In her recent *New York Times* article, Professor Deborah Tannen reminds us that apologizing is often seen by boys as a sign of weakness. She says—"

Murray pulled a pad from the packet he'd brought with him to the stage and began to read from it: " 'More men than women might resist apologizing, since most boys learn early on that their peers will take advantage of them if they appear weak. Girls, in contrast, tend to reward other girls who talk in ways that show they don't think they're better than their peers.' "

He put down the pad. "So we see that peer pressure seriously affects the way we speak to one another. Of course, as we mature and our awareness, competence, and self-esteem grow, we can become less dependent on peer approval. So after checking out the literature on this topic and chewing it over with my homies, I've come to the conclusion that I'll get better as I get older."

Sean leaped up and led the Crew's applause. Amber rolled her eyes at me, but De was smiling proudly at her man. Murray returned the grin, then held up his hands and signaled for silence. "I'm not through." From the mess on his lectern he pulled out two packages and carried them across the stage to Dionne.

"What is this?" she asked.

"Chocolates," said Murray, "perfume, and . . ." He reached into his back pocket, withdrew his wallet, and flipped it open. The cameraman panned in and, on the monitor above the stage we saw a color snapshot of Dionne.

"Tscha!" She snapped her fingers. "It's number forty-eight, 'Buy her little presents, like a small box of chocolates or perfume,'" she recited. "And number fifty-two, 'Let her see that you carry a picture of her. Oh, Murray, you read the book!"

"Okay, now I'm done," Murray instructed Sean. And we all started hollering and applauding. Mr. Hall stood up, still clapping, and said, "That was an excellent segment. Thank you, both. Okay, Amber and Mrs. Hanratty. You're up next."

I pulled out my cellular and dialed Daddy's number. He picked up on the third ring. "What?" he said.

"Hi, Daddy. It's me. Are you and Aldo's dad on your way?"

"We're almost there. John and I are watching golf. The PBA Senior Tour—"

"His name is *Jah*-nee, Daddy. As in Gianni Versace," I said, pronouncing it as Aldo had taught me.

"Great. Well, you can tell him that when you see him. I'm sure he'll be glad to know. Uh-oh, Chi Chi got a birdie. See you soon." He hung up.

I snapped shut my cell phone. Sometime during the De and Murray show, Dr. Kharkomoun of the Surgical Enhancement Imaging Institute had entered the cable studio. Now she directed the setting up of her computer onstage while Amber led Mrs. Hanratty to one of the swivel chairs.

I looked across the aisle at Aldo. He and his mother were now comfortably engaged in Italianate conversation. For his video debut, my hottie had donned Dolce & Gabbana, and I could hardly tear my eyes away from the festive skinny jersey draping his lean torso. He must have sensed my gaze. He glanced over his shoulder suddenly and gave me this blazingly noble grin. A moment later he was at my side.

"You look beautiful," he said, gently brushing back a stray strand of hair from my face. "You must meet my mother, no?"

"No," I agreed. "I mean I'd actually love to—she's a raging Betty and brutally haute couture—but I can't risk it, Aldo. I have to think of my show. Accusations of bias or partiality could seriously injure the segment."

"And my father, he will arrive with your father, yes?"

I nodded affirmatively. "They're in the limo now, catching a televised golf game. Then they're slated to hang in the reception area until called. Daddy is way overbooked," I explained. "But with a laptop and cell phone he can take care of business until it's time for his cameo. Plus, that way, your mom and dad don't have to see each other."

"Excuse me. Hello. Cher, Aldo. I have a show to do here." Amber's crabby announcement was followed by this crackling noise as if someone had bitten into a mammoth potato chip. It was her stiffly sprayed hair hitting the mike.

Against excellent advice, the willful one had decided to reprise her anchorgirl look. It was an unfortunate decision, although the flaming shade her colorist had gone with did, coincidentally, match the studio's swivel-chair upholstery. De and I had strenuously tried to talk her out of it. Now a sound engineer scurried onto the stage to examine her lapel mike.

Amber turned her head, and the static exploded again. "It's your hair," the sound man said, shaking his head like a troubled physician. He unpinned the microphone from the sequined collar of her green chemise. "Can you use the lectern mike instead?"

Amber nodded cautiously, crackle-free at last. "Good morning, everyone. Hi. My name is Amber—" she began.

Everyone went, "Hi-iii, Amber."

Aldo did quick but mellow lip service to my cheeks, then scooted back to sit beside his excellently groomed designer mom.

"Today I'm going to report on the fascinating field of cosmetic surgery," Amber began. The sequined trim on her gangrenous dress was a big mistake. Under the glaring studio lights, she flashed like a tour bus full of camera buffs every time she moved. Some of her audience had already resorted to sunglasses and tennis visors.

Tai slid over to fill Aldo's vacant spot beside me. She took my arm and squeezed it. "How dope is this? We're on television!" she whispered excitedly. "And how radiant is Amber?"

"Blindingly," I said. "I tried talking sequin sense to her, but would the girl listen?"

"Tai, do you mind?" Amber glowered at us.

"Oh, stab me repeatedly," Tai called out. "I was totally complimenting you!"

Amber cleared her throat. "Surgical enhancement is a multibillion-dollar industry in our nation," she read from a three-by-five card. Then smiling into the camera she added, "And that is due in no small part to the support of the PTA and student body of Bronson Alcott High School. I think we can all be proud of that. Come on, put your hands together. Let's hear it for us."

There was this lame patter of applause, which Amber tried to bolster by going, "Come on, Mrs. Hanratty, clap. Let's get some blood moving through those wintry digits." But Dr. K. was getting Mrs. Hanratty into position in front of her computer, which the camera guy did this close-up of, while Amber continued.

"What is surgical enhancement?" she queried, flipping to another card. "Some call it rhinoplasty, but that actually refers only to nasal makeovers—and sounds grossly zoological anyway. You know, like rhino, hippo, elephanto. And while enhancement surgery *can* whittle down bloated body parts, it is so not just about reduction."

Dr. Kharkomoun tightly focused her camera on Mrs. Hanratty's face now. "Okay. That's good," she murmured, freezing the image on her computer screen. Enlarged on the overhead monitor, it was a disturbing sight and produced this icky feeling. Hanratty's hair, usually pulled back into a fierce bun, was all loose and scraggly and tucked behind her ears. Her seasoned face was brutally bare, frankly makeup free. You don't necessarily want to know your algebra teacher that well.

"Others call it plastic surgery," Amber went on, "which totally makes sense, if like all you're focusing on is the costs involved. Then yes, it may conceivably entail plastic. You would be surprised by how many people believe it's just this vain indulgence for the very rich. That is such a misconception. When people say plastic surgery is too expensive, my answer to them is 'Tell your father to get a second job.'"

"We're ready," Dr. K. interrupted Amber.

"Do what you have to do. I'll be with you in a minute," she responded. "I'm not finished with my intro yet. Now let's examine the phrase 'cosmetic surgery,' which is another way of describing this revitalizing corrective process. What exactly does 'cosmetic' mean? . . ." Amber continued reading from her cards, clueless that her audience was now glued to the Kharkomoun–Hanratty demo.

"If you had a magic wand and could change anything about your face," Dr. K. was saying to Mrs. Hanratty, "what would it be?"

Mrs. Hanratty cocked her head and studied her own image on the screen. Dr. K. took the computer wand from its holder. "This is our magic wand," she said. "It can mimic or approximate on screen only those procedures that our board-certified surgeons are capable of performing. So go ahead, give me your wish list."

"Well," Mrs. Hanratty began, in this surprisingly

timid voice, "I've never told anyone this, but I've always hated my ears. They're too big. They stick out."

Dr. K. took up her computer wand and went to work on screen. "Otoplasty, or reshaping ears, is a relatively simple procedure," she assured Mrs. Hanratty. "I don't think you'd want to do too much here, but how about this?"

A sprinkling of spontaneous applause greeted Dr. K.'s handiwork.

"Thank you," Amber said, believing the acclaim was for her. "I got that definition from *Merriam-Webster's Collegiate Dictionary,* which has over 180,000 entries developed from a state-of-the-art computerized un-abridged dictionary database—"

"And my eyes." Hanratty was warming to the process. "Lately I've noticed the puffiness under here." She pointed to her computer image.

Amber finally cut off her lecture and turned to see what was happening, unleashing a thousand points of light. She caught the tail end of Hanratty's comments: "I wish I didn't have those little bags under my eyes."

"Give me a break," Amber murmured. "Those aren't little bags, that's matched luggage."

"When we cut away excess skin and fat around the eyes," Dr. K. was saying, as her wand tap-tap-tapped the computer portrait, "to eliminate drooping upper eyelids and puffy bags below, like this, the procedure is called blepharoplasty."

Now even Amber was mesmerized. The face emerging on the monitor was fresh, exciting, and only vaguely familiar. But then, in addition to oto and blepharo tampering, a touch of rhino, and facial implants to maximize Mrs. H.'s minor chin, the doctor illustrated what a rhytidectomy, or face-lift, could do.

When the before-and-after shots appeared on the monitor, there was this collective gasp. The transformation was beyond heartening.

Gripping her gold box of Godiva chocolates and the petite flask of Chanel, De squiggled onto the bleachers between Tai and me. "I never realized what choice bones Mrs. Hanratty had under all those wrinkles. No wonder she's cranky."

"Really," Tai agreed. "I mean, like if your beauty was brutally buried beneath layers of flaccid flesh, wouldn't that make you want to hurl?"

"Projectilelly," I decided. "De, study that shot." I pointed to the after pic of Mrs. Hanratty. "Now add pouffy, casual, chin-length blond hair and a great set of dental laminates. Who does she look like?"

"Omigod! Cameron Diaz," De shrieked.

"Dr. Kharkomoun, thank you so much," Mr. Hall was saying. "Amber, Mrs. Hanratty—" He was shouting, actually, above the cries and clamor of a monstrously appreciative audience.

Dr. K. did this modest bow and began packing up her equipment. But Amber and Mrs. Hanratty stayed on-stage, throwing kisses and applauding back at their fans. I was way moved by Amber's triumph. When finally she'd milked the last accolade from the crowd and reluctantly retired from the platform, I gave her a big hug. "Excellent segment, girlfriend."

"Didn't you love how deftly I moved from my introduction into Dr. K.'s portion of the show?" she squealed.

"You mean when you made that evil remark about Hanratty's eyes?" I queried. "That was smooth."

"Face it, girlfriend"—Amber got all defensive—"if she stenciled a repeat LV pattern under those leathery orbs, the woman would definitely be toting Vuitton. But I'll say this for Mrs. H., her after photo was stunning. It looked so like a mature me."

"But enough about you," I said. "It's my turn now." I knew I was up next, even before Mr. Hall got back to his clipboard. "So are you ready?" I asked her.

Amber nodded stiffly. "I'll take care of Aldo's mother—"

"But wait for my signal, okay? Tai, when Amber beeps you, you bring Aldo's dad. And could you place my notes"—I handed them to her—"on the lectern to the left, please."

Tai took the papers and hurried off, murmuring, "You guys. This is sooo cool."

"Ariel, Alana, Baez, are we a go?" I asked.

They were fully prepared. So was Dionne.

"I'd rather use a hand mike than that lapel clip," I told the sound engineer. "I'm not just being ensembly overprotective," I explained, "although this fabric is so vulnerable. But some of my segment is going to involve audience participation, and I'll need mobility to, you know, go among the people."

A solid professional, he totally understood.

"Cher," Mr. Hall called, "are you all set?"

My team was on standby. I had so done my homework. My French tips were flawless; my hair gleamed
with highlights.

"Totally, Mr. Hall," I said, as my homies gave me a
heartfelt group hug. From the hive of their embrace, I
glanced at Aldo. He sent this significant grin my way and
offered an affectionate thumbs-up.

Chapter 13

"You've just tuned in to CNN," Dionne's voice boomed from the lectern. "The Cher News Network! Welcome to *The Cher Show!*"

Alana strolled across the narrow stage holding up this jammin' Applause sign Tai had created. It was done in the faux-Gothic lightning-bolt style of one of Ryder's favorite geriatric heavy-metal groups. The sign, and Alana in this teensy shimmering silver halter dress from Barneys, evoked earsplitting whistles and cheers.

"And now," De shouted into her mike, "give it up for *Cher!*"

Ariel tapped the cameraman. He swung toward the back of the studio. And, microphone in hand, I ran down the aisle between the bleachers, going, "Thank you! You guys are great! We've got a monster show lined up! Thank you, thank you!"

De and Alana were taking their bows as I ducked around the camera and hurried onto the stage. "Thank you, Alana and Dionne. We'll see more of them later. Aren't they the best?"

There was another round of applause. Then, at my signal, Alana turned her sign around. In Tai's Gothic script it said Enough Already. So people began to settle down as I continued.

"My first guest is a total giant in apparel. She's renowned throughout the world," I said, with a gracious sweeping gesture of my left arm, which I hoped Amber would notice.

Although she was standing close to Aldo's mom, my trusted friend was flapping her lips at Jesse Fiegenhut.

"Someone whose work is like literally close to us," I continued. "In fact, that amazing fabric cinching Alana's bodice right now was designed by this outstanding fashion notable." I swung open my arm again. And was once more bitterly ignored.

"Amber," I finally called, "could you like get over yourself and bring up my guest?"

She squinched her eyes at me. Then she did this Vanna White twirl and like displayed Simona Biagi. Aldo leaned over and said something to his mom, and she got up and waved. At which point, Amber grabbed her hand and tugged her toward the stage.

"Please help me welcome . . . Simona Biagi," I said.

"Let's hear it," Dionne shouted as Amber settled Simona into one of the swivel chairs. My awesome guest crossed her lengthy legs and shook out this lion's mane of streaky sandy hair endearingly reminiscent of Aldo's.

"Let's everybody help Cher welcome the internation-ally renowned fabric designer Simona Biagi to *The Cher Show!*" De urged.

Aldo's mom was decked out in a creamy Missoni frock with a major scarf of her own design knotted at her throat and augmented by a cluster of Pintaldi beads so chic they actually made the tangerine chair look good. As the sound man clipped on Simona's mike, she raised a wrist laden with chunky designer bracelets and saluted the audience with this clanking yet regal little wave.

Alana flipped her sign to Applause, and everyone went wild again.

"De, can you beep Tai for me?" I asked under cover of the commotion. "Tell her to bring Aldo's dad in here in two minutes, okay? But make sure she gives me two minutes. I hate to ask you," I added, just as the applause ended, "but Amber has proved viciously unreliable."

The remark resounded through the suddenly quiet studio.

"That is so bogus," Amber announced, rushing to De's deserted lectern. "I have tried to be helpful," she whined into the microphone, "bitterly exhausted as I am from having just completed a prime-time piece of my own. A segment that I know you'll all agree was chronic—"

"Thank you, Amber." De repossessed the lectern mike. "And now back to the host of our show—*Cher!*" I swung over to the swivel-chair area as Dionne eased the sequined one offstage.

"Simona Biagi, it is so choice to meet you," I said.

"Fabric is a huge part of, well, the fabric of our lives, isn't it? Let's see, now, Simona, you've lived in Italy for"—I shuffled through my cards but couldn't locate the info I was looking for—"like a really long time," I improvised, "and it was there that you established this monster reputation for creating fabrics that radically bust fresh in these chronic muted shades accessorized with vivid trim such as the sequins my esteemed colleague is wearing today—but way more attractive. But unlike your estranged husband, Gianni, you were born in America, right?"

The mention of her soon-to-be ex seemed to startle my knowledgeable guest.

"Never mind," I said reassuringly. "Actually I'm just way pleased that you agreed to come on the show." I got up and, hand mike in tow, moved toward the lectern. "In addition to being a renowned fabric designer, Simona Biagi just happens to be the mother of our new classmate, Aldo Belloguardia," I told my audience, "and to me, while career achievement is something we all strive for, producing a hottie as down as Aldo is true success."

"Let's hear it for Italy's brutal loss and our Baldwinian gain," De burst out unexpectedly. "Put your hands together for Aldo!"

Alana started to hoist the Applause sign again, but I tore it from her hands before it could trigger another raucous round of audience participation.

"Thanks, De and Alana. You've both been amazing." I handed back the sign and whispered for them to bail, which I have to say they did with these waves and smiles and just incredibly supportive courtesy.

When I turned back to my guest, her sophisticated mask had fully melted into this inspiring maternal smile. Simona Biagi was looking out into the audience at Aldo, and she was furiously aglow with pride.

"So I know that as a parent you want what's best for your child," I quickly followed up. "And I'd say that would have to include like sparing him unnecessary distress and possibly shielding him from the turmoil of adult issues he didn't cause and can't control. Trust me on this, Simona. We the privileged youth of Beverly Hills know, as few others can, how harsh even a fabulous adolescence can be. And I'm sure that Aldo's father feels exactly the same way. So come on, everyone, let's give a warm *Cher Show* welcome to Aldo's dad, Gianni Belloguardia!"

Without De or Alana's prompting, my audience displayed spontaneous enthusiasm. But Simona's face clouded ominously. She jumped to her feet, enraged, rigid.

I rushed to her. "Oh, please. You can't walk off my show. I'm not Geraldo. I wouldn't even know how to cope with such public rejection, let alone nurse it for publicity purposes. And I am so unskilled at groveling. I never grovel unless a friend's happiness is at stake. So please stay for Aldo's sake. Just think about it, okay?"

Led by Tai, Aldo's stately father strode onto the stage. He was all big-shouldered double-breasted Armani. Except for his red silk tie and matching pocket handkerchief, which bore the distinctive look of a Simona Biagi design. It was so poignant. I couldn't help but think how, even on the verge of losing her, Aldo's dad, whenever he patted his pocket hankie, would be pressing a piece of Simona to his heart.

He hadn't noticed his estranged wife yet. I hurried to intercept him. "Hi, I'm Cher, Mr. Belloguardia," I said. "I'm not just the host of this segment, I'm also an extremely close personal friend of your son. And I'd really appreciate it if you'd like just be totally open-minded for a few minutes. You know, try to put aside present conflicts and unresolved issues and see if you can stretch yourself in terms of tolerance. Kind of just go with the flow here. For the good of Aldo."

Gianni Belloguardia nodded as I spoke, then rewarded me with this def Aldoesque grin.

"Oh, thank you so much," I started to say.

My relief was abruptly impaired, however, when this deafening "Hah!" broke out. It was Aldo's mom. "Hah!" she cried again. "He doesn't even know what you are saying. He doesn't understand a word."

"*Tu?*" Gianni whirled to face Simona. "You!" The next thing I knew, they were heatedly arguing in Italiano. I assumed that she was translating what I'd said. But it was hard to tell.

There was a lot of noise and gesturing. Hands flew, shoulders shrugged, chins bobbed, eyes rolled. Then abruptly they both sort of threw themselves into adjoining swivel chairs, crossed their arms over their respective chests, and stared at me with angry expectation.

"Will Mr. Belloguardia understand what I'm saying?" I asked Aldo's mother.

Gianni nodded. "I understand. I know," he assured me.

"I will translate for him. Believe me," Simona said, "I will make him understand."

"That is so choice of you," I said, raising my arms above my head. "Come on, everyone, let's all thank the Belloguardias, Simona and Gianni, for being such good sports."

Alana, who had sat down next to Amber and De in the first row of the bleachers, jumped up and led the applause.

"Is this scene familiar?" I shouted above the fray, indicating the moody adults behind me.

Everyone went, "Way!" and "Brutally!" and "Tell me about it!"

"Family friction," I said. "It's not a pretty sight. And yet there are those among us who have managed not only to survive it but to thrive in spite of it. These are the people I'd like you—and Aldo's parents—to meet today."

Then I went out into the audience and did these mini-interviews with Baez, Jesse, Ariel, and three of our other peers who had killer custody success stories to relate.

I saved Annabell Gutterman for last because her tale so summed up my message. "In your own words, Annabell," I said, "could you tell us how you got a Porsche, a forty-eight-pair wardrobe of Jourdan, Blahnik, and Capezio pumps, your own gold card, spring break with five friends of your choice in a Gwathmey-designed condo at Cabo San Lucas, and so much more?"

"Yes, Cher, I'd be glad to," Annabell replied into the mike, shaking out the silky dark locks she had conditioned weekly by Art Luna, Jennifer Aniston's West Hollywood hair guru. "In three little words: my parents' divorce. Each of them wanted an exclusive on me, and they got into this bitter contest to woo me. It was so fabulous."

"But it must have been way difficult to be pursued by both of them. Didn't that like make your life just icky?"

"Well, yes, Cher, it reeked for a little while. But then this monster celebrity attorney got wind of my domestic dilemma and offered me her services. How excellent is that?"

"Frantically," I affirmed. "So then like you engaged your own attorney, this renowned and fully credentialed shark? Is that correct?" I glanced up at the Belloguardias. Simona had begun ferociously whispering in Gianni's ear.

"Yes, Cher, I did. And once she was on the scene representing my interests in the case, things took a serious turn for the better in my life."

"And would you say that your attorney was as celebrated and fierce as, say, my very own father?" I pressed on, "Who is, at this moment, waiting behind the scenes to step onto our stage, and who might even consider offering his services to our cherished homie, Aldo?"

A disturbing sound drew my gaze stageward again. It was the metallic clanking of Aldo's mom's Elsa Peretti and Paloma Picasso bracelets. Simona's hands were gesturing wildly, accessorizing her discussion with Gianni. I watched his elderly hottie features contort as he pondered the implications of Aldo having an attorney at his disposal. Especially one with Daddy's exalted reputation. Daddy has been described as a total blood-drawing pit-bull litigator.

"Thank you, Annabell," I said, signaling Tai to fetch Daddy. "And now we're going to take a tiny break. But don't go away or you'll miss a wicked musical moment. . . ."

At my cue, three of my closest friends hurried onto the stage and clustered around the lectern. "It's the Children of Divorce Girls' Chorus!" I shouted. And as I turned to confer with Aldo, Dionne led our posse in a spirited version of "Respect," that like started out: "D-i-v-o-r-c-e, find out what it means to me."

"So how do you think we're doing?" I asked my awesome Baldwin.

He took my face in his hands and planted a big noisy one on each cheek. "Cher, they are talking to each other," he said, eyes twinkling playfully. "So you can tell me how dope is that?"

"Frantically dope," I replied. "Now let's clarify your demands before Daddy arrives, okay?"

"*Uno.*" Aldo counted them off. "No more spying on me from the cars. *Due,* no one tells me what to say or not to say to the other one—"

"Aldo, are you totally sure you want to finish high school in Italy?" I interrupted.

149

"Sì, cara." He did that thing with my hair again, just touched it lightly, brushing a fallen strand back behind my ear. "Yes, Cher. I have there my friends, my language, my home, everything familiar and easier for me. But for the holidays, for school breaks, and for the summer, I want to be here with my mother and my new friends . . . and with you."

"Not necessarily in that order, right?" I teased.

Aldo laughed, but then his golden face went soft and serious. His dark eyes slowly swept my face, as if he was trying to memorize it, lock it into his head and heart. "Believe this. I want most of all, Cher, to be with you."

A round of applause roused me from our interlude. I ran back to the stage just as Tai led Daddy into the studio. "Come on, everyone, let's thank the Children of Divorce! Are they props or what?" I called out. My buds took their bow. I slapped a high five with each of them as they filed back to their seats.

"And now here's a man that—I have to say this—I totally love. A man who is not just a brutal humanitarian when it comes to my wants and needs but who furiously pursues liberty and justice for all of his clients. He's the Barracuda of the Bar, the Lethal Weapon of Litigation, and my personal full-out favorite attorney of record, Mel Horowitz. Please help me welcome . . . Daddy!"

Daddy sauntered to center stage. Suddenly Gianni leaped up and rushed toward him. He grabbed the faun suede lapels of the choice Joseph Abboud jacket I'd picked out for Daddy's appearance on my show. "My son he don't need—" Gianni sputtered.

"Doesn't," Simona called out, correcting him. "It's 'My son *doesn't* need,' Gianni."

"Come here! *Vieni!*" he commanded her, then diplomatically added, *"per favore, tesoro.* Please."

"Tesoro means 'treasure,'" Aldo's mom informed me as she strolled over to Daddy. "He calls me a treasure. Mel," she said, with this most radiant smile. "If I may call you that?" Daddy nodded permission. "Aldo, our son, has no need of a lawyer. Gianni and I have had a very fruitful discussion today." She turned to her husband. *"Non è vero?* It's true, yes?"

"È vero!" He nodded way emphatically. *"No avvocato, no legale.* It is not necessary."

"We believe we can work things out favorably for all concerned," Simona announced.

"And have you asked Aldo what he wants?" I interjected, offering her the mike, which she firmly pushed aside. "Because that's crucial here," I continued. "Although Aldo is technically a minor, his feelings, desires, and needs are way major to me and to all his buds at Bronson Alcott. With all due respect—I mean, Simona, I love your fabrics and Gianni, your labels are the bomb—but the two of you have like heinously dropped the integer from your separation equation."

"Cher, that was so well stated!" Mrs. Hanratty leaped to her feet. "Didn't you find it eloquent, Mr. Hall?" she shouted out.

"An interesting metaphor," he agreed.

"And so algebraic," Hanratty trilled. "Let's hear it for Cher!"

But I held up my hands. "No applause, please. We're almost finished. Let's hold it for my final guest. In the time-honored tradition of saving the best for last, I give you—and that's just a figure of speech—Bronson Alcott's too cool Tuscan hottie, Aldo Belloguardia!"

As the boy bounded onto the stage, the studio exploded in a deafening endorsement. Aldo stopped in his tracks, stunned. His parents, too, were furiously astonished at the quality and quantity of support their son had stirred. Even I felt choked.

I took Aldo's hand. "Daddy," I said, "this is my friend Aldo. And if he needs legal advice, which there is only the teensiest possibility of now, right?" I glanced significantly at Simona and Gianni. She nodded vigorously, then poked her husband and he joined in the frantic head-wagging. "Well, just in case, would you be willing to help him negotiate like this monster settlement, Daddy?"

"Who is this kid?" Daddy asked.

"My friend Aldo," I whispered. "I told you all about him, Daddy."

Studying Aldo's face with a puzzled look, Daddy stuck out his hand. Aldo took it. I placed my manicured digits over theirs. And we did this chronic three-way shake. "Oh, thank you, Daddy," I said, breaking free to buss his cheek gratefully.

He was still appraising my Baldwin. "You know, Cher, in a baseball cap and sweatshirt, this kid could be the identical twin of that pizza delivery guy."

"Whoops," I said. "What a brutal coincidence."

Then, in full view of our parents and peers, Aldo wrapped his arms around me and delivered a massive hug.

"Good job, Cher," Mr. Hall hollered. And Mrs. Hanratty scrambled up onto the bleachers and led my audience in a thunderous standing ovation.

Chapter 14

Aldo's farewell fiesta was a monster bender.
The bash at his mom's Brentwood palazzo frantically
rocked. Simona had invited practically the entire school.
Daddy and I drove up right behind Mr. Hall and Miss
Geist, who had brought along this mature babe in a little
black go-everywhere dress. She looked vaguely familiar
yet alien.

Daddy caught me studying the woman. "Isn't that
your math teacher?" he asked.

"Mrs. Hanratty? Duh, right, like if she found an
excellent rinse and had major surgical reconstruction," I
responded.

The trio was approaching our car as Daddy and I got
out. "I can't believe it," I gasped. "It *is* her."

"Introduce me," Daddy said. Then, without even

waiting for me, he marched over and stuck out his hand. "I'm Cher's father. I think we've met."

"Alida Hanratty," the majorly renovated creature announced.

I left Daddy conversing with the scholastic crew and followed the fashionable crowd into the house. The party was in full bloom. From the doorway, my eyes swept the festive site in search of Aldo. I found De and Amber instead. They were signing autographs in the entry hall. They hadn't even checked their coats yet.

As I started toward them, an excited ninth grader rushed between me and my homies. "Cher, Cher! I can't believe it's you, in person!" he gasped. "Can you sign this for me, please?" He handed me a legal document and a pen.

I've always basked in the rampant admiration of my peers. Actually, my entire posse is brutally bloated with esteem. But after Bronson Alcott's live news show aired, our ratings went right through the roof.

For a full week following our cable debut, we could barely make our way across the Quad. Squads of autograph hounds dogged our every step, demanding our signatures on yearbooks, tardy notes, detention hall slips, T-shirts, and body casts.

Now, although my hand was viciously cramped by pen abuse, I signed my name on the folded paper the young fan had thrust at me.

"It's my mom's first separation agreement," the boy confided with a proud smile. "You know, I felt like such a geek because when my folks split they were all 'Well,

155

we can work this out,' and 'Who needs lawyers?' and 'Let's be friends.' But after I told her about your show, she contracted this killer attorney, and now I've got a four-figure monthly allowance." He waved the auto- graphed document triumphantly. "It's all here. Thanks, Cher."

By that time De and Amber had spotted me.

"Excellent frock," Dionne hollered as we elbowed through the crush toward one another. "Calvin does a chronic bon voyage costume, doesn't he?" She was referring to the petite bronze velvet mini I'd selected for this bittersweet moment.

"Well, it doesn't reek," Amber, who was flocked in yet another hairy ensemble, generously conceded. She spun for me. "I picked up this vintage angora on Beverly Boulevard—the very venue we were once slated to browse."

Suddenly a stranger in huge dark glasses tore at the pilled sleeve of Amber's sweater dress.

"Thank you for validating my lid lifts. Without your excellent cable piece, I'd never have done this," the girl gushed, raising her dark glasses to reveal the kind of puffy sutured black eyes you mostly see on *Hard Copy* and *ER*.

De shrank back, shrieking, "Eeewww!"

But Amber—after roughly swatting the girl's hand off her sleeve—agreed to autograph her fan's credit-card receipt from the Surgical Enhancement Imaging Insti- tute.

"Have you seen Aldo yet?" I asked, craning my neck for a glimpse of my Baldwin.

"Not yet," De answered. "Amber and I were viciously mobbed the minute we hit the door."

"Dionne, you saved my life!" someone called. "I could totally not communicate with my main boo until I caught your segment. What time are you and Murray debating tomorrow?"

"We're arguing at noon on the patio outside the cafeteria," De responded. "And at two-thirty in the computer lab, and we're slated for a late afternoon replay at the polo field. You'll need a ticket, though— see Sean."

De took my arm and we inched forward through the throng. Up ahead, near the coat rack, Annabell was describing the terms of her parents' divorce to a rapt audience.

"Hey, Cher. Everyone, I'm sure you recognize Cher, the high-rated host of Bronson Alcott's best ever talk show. Hi, Dionne," she called out to us. "De, I heard you and Murray were taking your dramatic improvs on the road."

There was a burst of applause from the party guests surrounding Annabell. I gave them a little wave. De said, "Our televised point-counterpoint pulled such a monster response that Murray and I decided to do a lecture circuit demonstrating boy-girl debating techniques. So now," she explained, "our disagreements will be totally positive and way instructional. Don't miss them. Check with Sean about available seating."

"I am so moved," I said, hugging my homie. "De, isn't it jammin' to realize that our popularity quotient can actually rise?"

"I fully believed that we'd topped out long ago," De agreed, "but I guess you can never be too adored."

"If I see one more bandage or black-and-blue mark, I'm going to seriously spew," Amber announced, pushing her way through a flock of fawning fans.

"Yo, Cher!"

It was Ryder. With one clenched fist churning the air, he was skating down the circular banister of Simona's classic marble staircase. "Children of divorce rule!" he shouted.

"Glad you liked my episode," I said graciously as he landed in a heap at our feet.

"Yeah, so can I have your autograph, too? Like on a blank check."

"I furiously fail to understand what Tai sees in you," Dionne said sharply.

"Then you'll be cheered to hear that Tai and me are splitski," Ryder announced, struggling to his wheeled feet. "We broke up after viewing your big cable segment. So basically it's like all your fault."

"Not even!" De responded. "Ryder, that is frantically unfair—"

He cut her off abruptly. "Right. Well, I'm wounded, dude. Anyone got a tissue or something?"

De and I exchanged looks. We were way astonished at Ryder's display of vulnerability.

As De rummaged through her bag for a tissue, I tried to comfort the heartbroken boy. "Forgive our callousness, Ryder. We had no idea how sensitive you were. Or that losing Tai would affect you so deeply that you'd feel like crying."

"Me cry over getting dumped?" said the surprised slacker. "As if!"

"Well, you did ask for a tissue, didn't you?" De demanded.

"Yeah, well, I did gash my arm doing a flip off the steps, didn't I?" Ryder answered, pointing a torn-up elbow at us. "And I do need something to suck up spilled blood, don't I? I mean, Tai was dope and all. And like I'm definitely probably gonna miss her. But I'm way used to being spurned by babes."

De held out a tissue, but Amber grabbed it before Ryder could and began dabbing at his elbow. "Did you catch my piece on plastic surgery?" she asked him. "Do you even know what an unsightly scar even a minor accident like this can inflict?"

De and I slipped away, leaving our t.b. bud to describe the miracles of collagen and dermabrasion to the wincing cadet.

"Speaking of heartbreak, how are you holding up, girlfriend?" Dionne asked as we tried to move anonymously through the dining room and head toward the back of the house.

"Well, I have to say that while I'm bereft knowing that Aldo is leaving tomorrow," I confided, "I'm seriously psyched at how well Simona and Gianni are working out their differences. Life will be way more choice for my hottie now. I mean, feuding parents are easy to manipulate but bitterly painful to live with."

"Aldo's parents have made up?" De shooed away a couple of kids with autograph books in their hands. "No signatures beyond the entry hall," she told them,

159

though we kept smiling and nodding to frenzied fans all the way to the back patio doors.

Through the French doors we could see the main party venue—sloping lawns, marble statues, and a monster buffet at which plate-holding power snackers were already lined up.

"It's not a full-out reconciliation," I explained, "but negotiations look promising."

Summer, Baez, and Janet called to us as we stepped outside. They came running toward the patio, all outfitted in identical dresses only in three different pastel hues. It was a cute little T-shirt knit, but multiplied by three it looked like a Gap rack. What a vicious debacle, I thought, to show up at the gala of the season wearing the same costume as your best friends. My heart went out to them.

"Have you heard about us?" Janet asked.

"No, but how brutally embarrassing," I said, with furious compassion.

"Not even!" Baez balked. "It's the totally coolest thing. Not only are we doing this fiesta but we've also got a sweet sixteen and two bar mitzvahs booked."

"Doing this fiesta? Excuse me?" De said.

"The Children of Divorce Girls' Chorus," Summer explained. "We've been getting calls ever since the *Alcott Buzz* show aired."

"We're singing here later," Baez said.

"Only we're not the Children of Divorce anymore," Janet added. "We've changed our name. We're Fractured Families now."

160

"That's why you're all wearing the same garments!"

"Duh," said Summer.

"That is so wicked!" I exclaimed. We slapped limp high fives all around. Then I asked, "Have you seen Aldo yet?"

"He was looking for you a couple of minutes ago," Baez said. "I think he and Murray are still out here somewhere," Baez said. "We're going inside to rehearse. Catch you later."

De and I began to saunter in the direction Baez had indicated. Suddenly Amber came huffing up behind us. "I just saw the most horrible thing," she gasped.

"Let me guess," De said. "Janet, Baez, and Summer identically ensembled?"

"Didn't you want to weep for them?" Amber shuddered, then said, "Ryder is considering a chemical peel. It's just a minor procedure to, you know, eliminate blemished, unevenly pigmented skin."

"That boy's needs are way beyond cosmetic," De offered.

"Well, he totally admired my garb," Amber said a bit defensively. "He was all 'Angora rules!' How cute is that? You know, Ryder is way more sensitive than people give him credit for."

"And so knowledgeable about fashion," said De.

"Poor Tai," Amber mused. "She's probably devastated about their breakup. She must be so alone."

"Not exactly," I said, pointing. Tai was standing on the food line, snuggling against the monster pecs of an infamous brawny bowhead.

"Leon!" De yelped.

"Don't even go there, girlfriend," I urged. "Just smile, wave, and be grateful. Be very, very grateful."

"That boy is so why bother," Amber assured her. "Well, I promised Ryder I'd bring him back a nibble. See you later," she called, heading for the buffet line.

"Okay, just breathe," I instructed Dionne, leading her away from Leon. We followed a flagstone path through an English garden. "Keep breathing," I was telling De. "Breathe in and chant, 'Been there.' Breathe out and say, 'Done that.'"

"Done what?" Murray rounded a corner and almost crashed into us. "Yo, Cher," he said, "I just left Aldo. He's been looking for you."

"Excellent," I said, trying to be frantically upbeat. But eager as I was to encounter the boy, my heart suddenly felt like lead. It was as if I'd eaten Lucy's pot roast or a chili dog at a random road diner.

Ever since we'd carved out the terms of Aldo's custody arrangement, I'd been in minor angst over this moment. It was time to say *arrivederci* to my honey. I would furiously miss him. I knew there would be an empty place in my life—a Baldwin-shaped hole that would just suck wind.

"He's right over there." Murray was pointing beyond a flowering hedge. But now my feet, clad in strappy bronze shoes, felt as heavy as my heart.

Dionne sensed my condition at once. "Good-byes blow chunks," she said, giving my arm a consoling squeeze.

"They totally spew," I agreed, working up a smile.

"Come on," Murray said. "I'll show you where he's at. Yo, Aldo," he called.

Dionne clamped a hand over his mouth. "Sorry, Cher. We're Audi," she announced.

Murray shook his face free. "Yo, you be wiggin', woman? Why you pressing my braces up against my lips like that?"

"Don't call me woman!" Dionne commanded. Then she took Murray's hand and dragged him away.

It was way comforting to hear their familiar dramatic duet again. I stood staring after them until their voices faded. And then, with a sigh, I turned around.

There he was, my golden hottie. His big dark eyes—in fact, his entire velvety face—lit up at the sight of me. "Chair," he said with this full-out grin. And I ran into his arms.

"Are you all packed? When do you take off?" I asked, not knowing what else to say. Which is so not me. My face was squished against his excellent squiggly-striped Versace polo shirt. "So you're going home."

"I go to Italy, yes." Aldo lifted up my chin and kissed me. His sculpted lips were warm and soft. And then he pulled back and studied my face for a long quiet time. "But home?" he said, gently tracing my face with his fingers. "Here is my home."

The words were like these delicate digits loosening the knot in my heart. I totally thought they deserved a monster hug. But I just stood there for a while, staring up at Aldo.

That was when I realized that I'd become a true journalist. Because as emotionally involved as I was in the warmth and sweetness of being in his arms, a part of me was repeating what he'd said: "Here is my home." And recalling the sound of his voice. And trying to memorize his face. I was standing apart and observing. Observing and remembering. Observing and recording. It was just like Mr. Hall said. I felt so investigative.

And then as Aldo and I walked hand in hand toward the buffet, where our posse was pigging, I got this total flash about a def new exposé I could do for the *Alcott Buzz*. It would require major trekking and massive research and arduous in-depth interviews.

Aldo squeezed my hand, and I glanced up at his furiously memorable face. We were both really smiling. But I was also viciously psyched about my next major article. I even had a title for it: "The Babes of Tuscany"—or maybe "Tuscany, Land of the Baldwins."

About the Author

H. B. Gilmour is the author of the best-selling novelizations *Clueless™* and *Pretty in Pink*, as well as *Clueless™: Achieving Personal Perfection; Clueless™: Cher's Guide to . . . Whatever; Clueless™: Friend or Faux; Clarissa Explains It All: Boys;* the well-reviewed young-adult novel *Ask Me If I Care;* and more than fifteen other books for adults and young people.